Welcome to

Gone to the stables

Jina

Sssh!! Studying—
please do not disturb!

Mary Beth

<u>GO AWAY!!!</u>

Andie

Hey, guys!
Meet me downstairs in the
common room. Bring popcorn!

Lauren

Join Andie, Jina, Mary Beth, and Lauren
for more fun at the Riding Academy!

And coming soon:

Feeling left out, Mary Beth headed down the path. She couldn't believe she'd told her new roommates she was signing up for the junior riding program. How could she have been so stupid?

And how was she going to get out of it?

"Hey, Red!" a voice shouted. Mary Beth looked over to see Andie riding Ranger in one of the outdoor rings.

Andie squeezed her legs against the bay's sides. When Ranger broke into a relaxed trot, she rose smoothly up and down.

"This is posting," Andie called. "In case you didn't know."

Mary Beth bristled. "Of course I know!" she called back. "And after I start lessons, I bet I'll be able to do that posting thing by the end of the first week!"

"No way!" Andie laughed as the horse trotted past Mary Beth. "I'll take that bet."

"Fine," Mary Beth said. *Take it and lose,* she added under her breath.

A HORSE
FOR MARY BETH

by Alison Hart

BULLSEYE BOOKS

Random House 🏠 New York

"I'll take *this* bed," Andie Perez announced. With a grin, she dropped her English saddle on the nearest mattress.

"But that's *my* bed," Mary Beth Finney protested. "My quilt and pillow are already on it."

Andie picked up Mary Beth's raggedy patchwork quilt and feather pillow and tossed them onto the bed by the hall door. "Not anymore," she sang out.

Mary Beth glared at her new roommate. Andie's long black hair fell to her shoulders in a wild mane, and she had a retainer on her already-straight-looking teeth. She was wearing a baggy T-shirt with a penguin on it that said I'M COOL.

Only it should say I'M MEAN, Mary Beth

1

told herself angrily. *What a creep!*

"And while I'm gone, don't even *touch* my saddle." Andie's dark eyes snapped as she left the room and disappeared down the hall.

"Rats!" Mary Beth threw herself facedown on the other bed. Since it was next to the door, she could hear giggles, shrieks, and pounding feet in the hall. A bed by the window would have been so quiet.

With a sigh Mary Beth stuffed the pillow under her chin. She'd only been at Foxhall Academy for two hours and already she hated it. How could she share a room with a snotty girl like Andie? And the worst thing was, she had two other roommates!

Andie was the only roommate she'd met so far, but someone else had already taken the other bed by the window. It had been carefully made up with a pink-flowered bedspread and matching dust ruffle. The fourth girl assigned to suite 4B hadn't shown up yet.

"Suite." That was a joke. The room was tiny, with four beds, four dressers, four desks, and *one* adjoining bathroom.

Mary Beth flipped onto her back and stuck the pillow over her face. Enrolling in a private girls' school in Maryland was a big mistake.

She'd just have to write her mother and tell her she was catching the first train home. Even sixth grade at Cedarville Elementary School with superstrict Mrs. Henderson would be better than Foxhall Academy.

"Hi!" a cheery voice called.

Mary Beth whipped the pillow off her face. A girl about her own age was staring down at her. She had a long honey blond braid, blue eyes, and a big smile. A stack of textbooks was propped under one arm.

"Hi," Mary Beth said, sitting up.

"I'm Lauren Remick, one of your roommates," the blond girl said as she sat on the edge of the mattress. She was wearing baggy shorts and a pink T-shirt. "And that's me over there," she added, pointing to the bed with the dust ruffle.

"I'm Mary Beth Finney and that *was* me over there." Mary Beth nodded toward the bed across from Lauren's—the one that had the smelly saddle on it. "Someone kicked me off it."

Lauren laughed. She had the kind of laugh that rose up and down like a music scale, and Mary Beth couldn't help but smile.

"That sounds like Andie," Lauren said, tossing her braid behind her shoulders. "I met her this summer when my parents and I came to visit the school. She's a little bossy."

"She's bossy, all right," Mary Beth muttered.

"Hey, I love your hair," Lauren said. "I've always wanted to be a redhead."

Mary Beth made a face and touched her wispy bangs. "Maybe we can trade sometime," she said, liking Lauren even more. She'd always been self-conscious about the color of her hair.

"So where's your Big Sister?" Lauren asked. All the sixth graders were assigned an older student to help them out on the first day of school.

Mary Beth sighed. "She's sick. The headmaster is trying to find me a new one. That's why I'm hanging around here."

Lauren shook her head. "That's too bad. My Big Sister, Eileen Berman, has been super. We got my schedule straightened out and picked up my books. My *real* big sister has been going to Foxhall for years, so I didn't have any trouble figuring out where my classes are. I've even checked out the stables already."

"Your sister goes here too? That's great."

Lauren nodded. "Yeah. She's a dancer, and I'm here for the riding program. How about you?" Jumping off the bed, Lauren went over to her desk and dropped her books on top.

"I'm here because the math and science courses are supposed to be so good. I like dance too, I guess. Only it's my first time away from home, so I'm a little—" Mary Beth flushed.

"Homesick?" Lauren gave her a big smile, and for the first time Mary Beth noticed how tiny her new roommate was. She'd look like a gawky giant next to her.

"I've been to riding camp before," Lauren said. "But that was only for a month. Stephanie, my sister, says she used to get homesick sometimes. But now she's a junior, and she can't wait to get away from our parents."

Just then Mary Beth's stomach growled. She quickly slapped her hand over it. "I wish my Big Sister would hurry up and get here so she could show me where the cafeteria is."

"Oh, that's easy." Lauren gestured for Mary Beth to come over to the window. Their suite was on the fourth floor of Bracken Hall, their dorm. When Mary Beth looked outside, she was able to see most of the campus.

Below their window was a grassy central courtyard with buildings clustered around it. Since the school had been founded in the late 1800s, Old House, the administrative building, looked like a clapboard farmhouse that had been added on to many times. Next to it was the ivy-covered stone library. Beyond the library Mary Beth could see the modern gymnasium and dance studio. Two other dorms and a classroom building also surrounded the courtyard.

Mary Beth watched the students and parents hurrying across the grass. A few upper-school girls were sunbathing on towels or sitting on benches shaded by oaks and dogwoods. It was such a beautiful campus, Mary Beth couldn't help but feel a ripple of excitement.

"The cafeteria is that long building on the right," Lauren said, "the one with the white shutters between the two dorms. It's named Eaton Hall, but Eileen said everyone calls it Don't Eaton Hall. The food is really lousy."

Mary Beth laughed. "Well, I'm so hungry right now, I could 'eaton' anything."

"I had lunch already, but I can go over

again with you," Lauren said. "Hey," she added suddenly, "look at that."

Below them a white stretch limousine was cruising up the drive. It stopped in front of their dorm.

"Oooo. Maybe the president of the United States' daughter is coming to Foxhall," Mary Beth said as she leaned forward to see who got out.

A uniformed driver jumped out of the limo and jogged around to the passenger door. But before he reached it, the door swung open. A girl who looked about eleven climbed out, dragging a small suitcase with her. The driver tried to take the suitcase, but the girl yanked it from his reach.

As if she was in a hurry, the girl pushed past the driver and marched into the dorm. The driver shook his head, then slowly opened the trunk of the limo. He pulled out two huge matching designer garment bags and a small trunk.

"Wow. Can you imagine having your own chauffeur?" Lauren asked.

"And look at all that luggage," Mary Beth added with a low whistle. "I bet she'll hog all the closet space. I wonder which lucky suite is going to get stuck with *her*."

A sharp rap behind them made the two turn away from the window. The girl with all the bags was standing in the doorway. Her gleaming black hair was pulled back in a tight knot. She had golden eyes and smooth chocolate-colored skin. Both hands clutched the handle of the small suitcase.

"Hi. I'm Jina Williams," she said without a smile. "And if this is suite 4B, I'm your new roommate."

2

"This is 4B," Mary Beth said, taking in the girl's neat white jeans and expensive tennis shoes.

"Well, come on in." Lauren bounced across the floor and took Jina's suitcase. "There's only one bed left."

"That's okay." Jina's eyes darted toward the hallway. When the chauffeur came to the door carrying the trunk, she nodded for him to set it down.

"Leave the rest of my things downstairs, please," she told him.

The chauffeur frowned. He was a handsome black man in his late fifties. "Your mother told me to stay until—"

"Please leave them downstairs. Then you can go."

The chauffeur shrugged. "Whatever you say, Miss Williams." He shook his head and left the room, muttering, "But your mother's not going to like it."

Bending down, Jina dragged the trunk closer to the dresser at the foot of her bed. Mary Beth wondered why the girl's mother hadn't come to the school with her. Her own parents had left just half an hour ago after a million hugs good-bye.

"That's the only closet," Mary Beth told Jina, pointing to the old-fashioned wardrobe between her and Lauren's beds. "And there's not much space left."

Jina shrugged. "No problem."

"Would you like us to help you bring up your other suitcases?" Lauren asked.

"No."

"Then how about lunch?" Mary Beth suggested.

"I ate, thanks." Jina bent down and fiddled with the trunk's lock. When the lid opened, she reached in and took out a bridle.

Lauren's eyes widened. "You're a horse person too!"

Mary Beth groaned silently. If Jina, Lauren, and Andie were all in Foxhall's riding program,

10

then she'd really be the odd one out. She'd been terrified of horses since she was five years old.

"Yep." Without looking up, Jina pulled a tall black boot from her trunk and wiped off a speck of dust with her sleeve.

Mary Beth looked at Lauren and raised her eyebrows. Jina wasn't very friendly. She wondered which roommate would be worse: Jina Williams or Andie Perez.

"Well, we'll see you later," Lauren said.

"See you," Mary Beth echoed as she followed Lauren out the door. When they got into the hall, both of them let out their breath.

"Whew! That girl sure is snobby," Mary Beth said.

"Maybe this is her first time away from home too," Lauren offered.

"I doubt that. I mean, she had a chauffeur bring her to school."

Lauren shrugged. "Oh, that's not so unusual for Foxhall. The governor of Maryland's daughter is a senior, and she always arrives in a limo. Lots of girls at Foxhall are pretty rich," she added as they clattered downstairs to the first floor. "But not me and Stephanie."

And certainly not me, Mary Beth thought.

Bracken Hall had four floors of suites. The first floor had a common room where the girls could hang out. It was filled with comfortable chairs, books, a TV, a stereo, and a microwave. Next to the common room was an apartment for Ms. Shiroo, the teacher who was also one of the dorm mothers.

As Mary Beth pushed through the heavy double doors and stepped outside, humid air blasted in her face. It was a typical Maryland September.

"Mary Beth Finney, you're just the person I want to see." Mr. Frawley, the headmaster of Foxhall Academy, was bustling across the courtyard. He was wearing a tan suit, and his pant legs flapped against his skinny calves. As he came toward the two girls he pulled a handkerchief from his shirt pocket and dabbed beads of sweat from his red face.

"I've found a new Big Sister for you, Miss Finney," Mr. Frawley said when he reached them. "Her name is Christina Hernandez. She'll meet you in your dorm room in forty minutes." Then the headmaster turned and headed in another direction. "Ingrid Larsen! You're just the person I want to see!" he called to an older girl crossing the courtyard.

"He's pretty strange, isn't he?" Lauren said to Mary Beth. "But you're lucky. Christina Hernandez is my sister's roommate. You'll like her."

Mary Beth nodded.

"Hey," Lauren added, "before we go to the cafeteria, can we stop by the stables?"

"The stables?" Mary Beth repeated nervously.

"It will just take a second," Lauren said. "The dressage coach is going to exercise one of the school horses. This horse is my very favorite, and I'm hoping the director will assign her to me."

"But I only have forty minutes for lunch," Mary Beth protested weakly.

"Oh, you'll have lots of time." Lauren's mouth tilted down in a pretend pout. "Don't you want to see all the horses?"

No, thanks, Mary Beth wanted to say, but she smiled instead. She liked Lauren. Maybe if she acted as though she liked horses too, they could become good friends. "Okay," Mary Beth said.

"Great!" Lauren took off across the courtyard at a fast walk. Mary Beth had to work hard to keep up with her, even though the blond girl was tiny. The two of them passed through the stone archway connecting the library with the administration building, then headed up a shady hill.

On the right was a big indoor arena where riders exercised the horses in bad weather. On the left were two outdoor rings, the pastures, and the stable.

"Just wait until you see Whisper," Lauren said excitedly. "She's little—only about fifteen hands—but when she starts to work on her dressage movements, she's pure poetry."

Mary Beth stopped to catch her breath. "Lauren, I hate to sound stupid, but what is *dressage*?"

"You mean you're not a rider?" Lauren looked completely shocked.

Mary Beth bit her bottom lip. Everyone she'd met so far at Foxhall Academy was obviously crazy about horses. If she admitted to Lauren how scared she was of them, they might not ever be friends.

"I know a little about horses, but not all that dressage stuff," she said finally.

"Oh." Lauren shrugged and started walking again. "I'll explain it to you sometime."

Mary Beth sighed gloomily as she trudged behind Lauren. I *really do love animals*, she wanted to tell her new roommate. *It's just that when I was five years old, a horse bucked me off, then stepped on me. I was in the hospital for a long time, and ever since I've had nightmares about riding.*

"Look, there's Whisper!" Lauren exclaimed, running toward the stable. It was a horseshoe-shaped building of about forty stalls. The roof hung over the stalls, making a shaded walkway. Each stall had Dutch doors that were open at the top. In the middle of the horseshoe girls were bathing horses and walking them in a grassy courtyard. Other girls were grooming horses tied under the overhang. Still more horses hung their heads over the bottom stall door.

Mary Beth had never seen so many horses in one place in her life. She gulped. What if they all got loose and stampeded?

"Over here!" Lauren called. She was standing by a stall, patting a red horse.

Mary Beth took a deep breath. *Okay*, she told herself. That horse has the same color hair as mine. She can't be all bad. Shoving her hands deep in her shorts pockets, she walked

15

toward Lauren, who was talking baby talk and kissing the horse on the nose.

"Whisper, this is my new roommate, Mary Beth," Lauren said. "Mary Beth, this is Whisper. I got to ride her this summer when I was here for a clinic."

Whisper swung her head around to look at Mary Beth. She had a white strip between her big brown eyes that ran almost to her nose. When Mary Beth gingerly patted the horse's velvety face, Whisper shook her head and snorted. Globs of grain flew from her mouth. Mary Beth grimaced as she wiped the gooey stuff off her bare arms. "She's really pretty. A redhead, too," she tried to joke.

"The color's called chestnut," Lauren explained. "But if the horse is reddish with a black mane and tail—like the one that Andie's holding over there—that's called bay."

"Andie's here?" Mary Beth spun around. Immediately she caught sight of the tall girl's wild dark hair. She was leading the bay horse down the walkway toward them.

"And there's Jina. Jina!" Lauren called, waving.

Jina was also heading toward them, carrying her bridle and a wooden box. When she saw

Lauren and Mary Beth, she came over to Whisper's stall.

"Jina, this is Andie, our other roommate," Lauren said.

"Hey! What do you know!" Andie exclaimed. "How exciting. All the roomies here at one time!" She halted her horse right in front of Mary Beth. It was tacked up with an English bridle and saddle, and it was *huge*.

Trying to get away from the animal, Mary Beth took a step backward, only to feel Whisper's nose pressing against her shoulder blades.

Andie grinned at Jina. "I saw you drive up in that cool limo. You must be filthy rich, huh?"

Jina ignored her and turned to Lauren.

"Is the chestnut horse yours?" she asked.

Lauren shook her head. "I wish. She belongs to the school."

Mary Beth could feel Whisper's lips playing with the back of her shirt. Beads of sweat appeared under her already-damp bangs. She had to move. But Lauren was on one side, Jina was standing in front of her, and Andie and her horse were on the other side.

She was trapped.

"How about you, Red?" Andie leaned

toward Mary Beth. "Do you ride too?" she asked. At the same time the bay's head swiveled around, his nose level with Mary Beth's face.

"Uh, sure," she stammered. "I ride all the time. At home," she added quickly. She'd never admit how scared she was. All she had to do was keep cool until the beast moved away.

Andie was looking at her with narrowed eyes. "So you're not in the riding program here?" she asked.

Mary Beth froze as the bay snuffled her chin. *Stay cool,* she told herself. Then the horse suddenly opened his mouth. All she could see were two rows of inch-long teeth.

Huge teeth about to sink into her flesh!

3

Throwing her arms in front of her face, Mary Beth screamed.

"Will you shut up!" Andie reached forward and clapped her hand over Mary Beth's mouth. "You'll scare the horses!"

With a snort the big bay shied sideways. "Easy, Ranger," Andie crooned.

Mary Beth stumbled backward against the stable wall and slid to the floor. When she dared to look up, she saw Jina, Lauren, and Whisper staring at her. Jina's arms were folded, and she was looking at Mary Beth as if she were a Martian.

"Are you all right?" Lauren crouched beside her. "Did he bite you?"

Andie snorted. "Ranger didn't touch her. He was just yawning. I'd say Mary Beth has a bad case of the scaredy-cats."

"I do not," Mary Beth snapped as she jumped to her feet. "In fact, I'm signing up for the junior riding program."

Andie burst out laughing. "Sure you are," she said. With a wave of her fingers she led the bay into the sunny courtyard.

"Jerk," Mary Beth muttered. Twisting around, she brushed the dirt and straw off the seat of her shorts.

"Don't pay any attention to Andie," Lauren said. "It's great you're signing up for the riding program. Why didn't you tell me before?"

Mary Beth shrugged. "I was just waiting to talk to my Big Sister about it," she lied.

Just then a silver horse van roared up the drive.

"Superstar's here!" Jina said, a huge smile lighting her face. Dropping her box and bridle on the ground, she jogged to the end of the walkway.

"Superstar?" Mary Beth asked Lauren.

Lauren's mouth dropped open as she stared after Jina. "Wow, what a dope I am!" she exclaimed, knocking herself on the forehead with her palm. "She must be *Jinaki* Williams. Last year she and her horse, Superstar, were the top horse and rider for the Children's Working Hunter Division. And she's our roommate! Can you believe it?"

"Gee, that's great," Mary Beth murmured. She didn't have the foggiest idea what Lauren was talking about.

The van screeched to a halt and the driver jumped out. "Hello, Miss Williams!" he called. "Where do you want this horse?"

"Third stall to the left of the office," said a pretty older woman as she came up to Jina's side. "We'll put him there until the new barn's finished."

The woman's tan face was wrinkled from years of being in the sun, and her gray-streaked hair was pulled back in a ponytail. Mary Beth recognized the woman from her visit to Foxhall with her parents last summer. She was Mrs. Caufield, the director of the riding program.

"I've just *got* to see Jina's horse!" Lauren said excitedly. She ran to join the growing crowd of girls clustered around the van.

Mary Beth let out her breath. It was hard to believe how everybody could get so excited over a huge four-legged animal with big teeth and a little brain.

But when the driver opened the van door and began to lead Superstar down the ramp, even Mary Beth had to admit he was beautiful. The sun glimmered off his gray dapples, and when he reached the ground, he pranced proudly in a circle like a horse from a Black Stallion book.

As she watched the girls fuss over Superstar, Mary Beth's stomach growled hungrily. She'd better hurry if she was going to grab a sandwich before meeting Christina. And it didn't look as though Lauren would be going to the cafeteria with her now.

Feeling a bit left out, Mary Beth headed down the path toward the school buildings. She couldn't believe that she had told her new roommates she was signing up for the riding program. How could she have been so stupid?

And how was she going to get out of it?

"Hey, Red!" a voice shouted. Mary Beth looked over to see Andie riding Ranger in one of the outdoor rings. She was wearing tight pants, tall black boots, and a riding helmet.

Andie squeezed her legs against the bay's sides. When he broke into a relaxed trot, she rose smoothly up and down.

"This is posting," Andie called. "In case you

didn't know, Freckle-Face Finney."

Mary Beth bristled. "Of course I know!" she called back. "And after I start lessons, I bet I'll be able to do that posting thing by the end of the first week!"

"No way." Andie laughed as the horse trotted past Mary Beth. "I'll take that bet."

"Fine," Mary Beth said. *Take it and lose,* she added under her breath as she continued down the hill toward the dorm. Forget the sandwich. It was time to meet Christina and find out how to change her schedule. She'd drop her dance class and sign up for riding.

If she didn't, Andie would keep taunting her, and Jina would keep giving her those funny looks. Even Lauren might like her better if they could ride together.

That means I have to learn how to ride, Mary Beth decided. *No matter what.*

"Boy, I sure wish Frawley would shut up so we could go back to the dorm and take off these stupid blazers," Andie whispered to Mary Beth.

For the first time that day, Mary Beth agreed with her roommate. The navy blue blazers the students had to wear to dinner were hot and itchy. She hated them, too.

It was seven-thirty, and Andie and Mary Beth were seated next to each other at one of the long dining tables in the cafeteria. They'd just finished their "Welcome to Foxhall Dinner," and the headmaster was droning on and on about Foxhall traditions and school spirit.

Lauren and Jina were sitting together on the other side of Mary Beth. All night long, Lauren had been talking to Jina about riding. Mary Beth couldn't help feeling jealous. She and Andie hadn't had much to talk about at all. Mary Beth had tried to tell her about Cedarville and her old school, but the dark-haired girl just seemed bored.

"And now I'd like to introduce the faculty of Foxhall Academy," Frawley said.

Mary Beth sat straighter, trying to see each of her teachers as he or she was introduced.

"Mr. Harold Cochran, math," Frawley said, pointing to a plump man with thinning hair.

Mary Beth had met Mr. Cochran when she and Christina had changed her schedule. He seemed really neat.

"Look at that dopey bow tie he's wearing," Andie whispered in her ear.

Mary Beth turned in her seat. "Shhh," she

said, frowning. "I'm trying to hear."

"Excu-u-u-se me," Andie said in a snotty voice, but after that she kept quiet.

After all the teachers had been introduced, Mr. Frawley invited the students and faculty to mingle while they munched on bite-size pastries from the buffet table at the end of the room. Mary Beth left the table quickly, eager to talk to her new teachers. But after half an hour of mingling, she began to feel overwhelmed.

She scanned the cafeteria, looking for Lauren. Finally she spotted her by the exit. She was standing next to a tall girl with tan legs and silky, honey gold hair. Christina Hernandez, Mary Beth's Big Sister, was with them.

Mary Beth quickly walked over, glad to see some familiar faces. "Hi," Lauren said when Mary Beth came up to them. "Meet my real big sister, Stephanie."

"Hi," Mary Beth greeted the blond girl. "And hi, Christina. Thanks again for helping me get my books and stuff this afternoon."

"No problem," Christina said, smiling. She was smaller than Stephanie, with jet black, chin-length hair. Gold hoops dangled from her earlobes.

Jina and Andie joined the group just as everyone was leaving, and Lauren made more introductions.

"Boy, am I ever ready to get out of here," Andie grumbled as they stepped out the door. "If I have to talk to one more teacher, I'm going to puke."

"Well, if you girls are going back to the dorm, Christina and I will walk you across the courtyard," Stephanie offered. "It's getting dark, and we wouldn't want you to run into Sarah." She gave Christina a knowing look.

"Who's Sarah?" Mary Beth asked.

"You mean you guys haven't heard about her?" Christina asked in a shocked voice.

Andie, Jina, and Mary Beth all shook their heads. Lauren nodded gravely. "I have," she said. "You told me when you came home from break last year."

"So tell the rest of us," Andie said impatiently.

Stephanie started down the steps. "Sarah is the school ghost," she said as the girls walked toward the administration building. "And when the moon is full, you can see her crossing the courtyard."

Mary Beth paused in front of the stone

arch and looked up. The moon was full *tonight*, she realized suddenly. But right now it was under a cloud.

"Sarah Pendleton was a student at Foxhall—just like us," Christina said, stopping next to Mary Beth. Her dark eyes were sparkling. "Only she was here way back in the 1800s."

"So what happened to her?" Jina asked.

"Well, one night Sarah snuck out of her dorm wearing only her nightgown and shawl," Stephanie said in a low voice. "The next day no one could find her. When the teachers went hunting for her, all they found was her torn shawl—covered with blood."

Mary Beth inhaled sharply. "Blood?"

Stephanie nodded. "They never found Sarah. The legend says she roams the campus because she wants her shawl."

Just then the moon peeked out from behind a cloud, casting eerie blue shadows around the arch.

Mary Beth shuddered.

"So was she murdered or what?" Andie demanded.

"No one knows," Christina said. "But maybe you guys can figure it out." Stephanie grinned slowly as she looked at the room-mates.

"Us?" they chorused.

"Sure." Stephanie's brows lifted. "You're standing right at the spot where they found her tattered, bloody shawl. And since there's a full moon tonight, Sarah's ghost should be along any minute to get it!"

Mary Beth, Andie, and Jina stared at the spot on the ground where Sarah had met her doom.

Mary Beth shivered. She didn't believe in ghosts, of course, but the story the older girls had told them certainly was spooky. Even Andie was quiet for once.

Suddenly Lauren clapped her hands to her mouth and started giggling.

"Gotcha!" Stephanie crowed. Then she and Christina started laughing, too.

"Real funny," Andie said, hands on her hips. "So funny, I'm going back to the dorm."

"I'll go with you. Nice meeting you, Christina and Stephanie," Jina said politely. She smiled briefly, then hurried after Andie.

"Well, *I* thought the story was funny."

Lauren said with a giggle.

"Me too," Mary Beth chimed in, afraid to admit she'd been scared.

Stephanie and Christina turned to go. "See you later, kids," Stephanie said as they headed toward the dorm together. "We've got gossip to catch up on."

Lauren and Mary Beth watched as the two older girls walked across the courtyard.

"I hate it when she calls me and my friends *kids*," Lauren said, frowning.

"She's just teasing," Mary Beth said, happy that Lauren considered her a friend. "Like she did with the dumb ghost story."

"Yeah," said Lauren. "I guess I'm kind of lucky to have Stephanie here at Foxhall with me. Even if she's a pain sometimes."

Maybe if I had a sister living in the same dorm as me, I wouldn't have to worry about getting lonely, Mary Beth thought. But her own sister, Tammy, was only two and drooled a lot. Mary Beth suddenly started feeling homesick again. Maybe later, when her roommates were asleep, she'd write a letter to her family.

Dear Mom and Dad,
I know it's only my first day here, but I

*miss you and Reed and Benji and Tammy so
much! Foxhall is okay, but I want to come
home. Please send me a train ticket so I can
leave this Saturday. I'll explain everything
to you when I get back to Cedarville.*

*Hugs and kisses to Benji, Reedy, and
Tammy.*

*Make sure Benji takes good care of all of
my pets, especially Dogums.*

Love,

Mary Beth

P.S. Don't forget the train ticket.

Setting down her pencil, Mary Beth held
her letter up to the moonlit window, trying to
read what she'd written.

It was very late, and her roommates were
asleep. Ms. Shiroo, the dorm mother, had told
them good night almost two hours ago since
lights out was at ten o'clock for the sixth
graders.

But Mary Beth couldn't sleep. Tomorrow
was her first day of classes—*and* her first riding
lesson.

How had she gotten herself into such a
mess?

With a sigh, she folded the letter and slid it

in the envelope. She was starting to lick the flap when a flash of white in the courtyard caught her attention. She leaned forward in the chair and pressed her face against the glass.

The moon had tinted everything in shades of blue. Mary Beth scanned the courtyard and the dark school buildings. Nothing.

Wait! She frowned. Under the stone arch something was swaying in the shadows. It was tall and white, like a person wearing a sheet. Or was it a ghost?

That's crazy, Mary Beth told herself. The spooky story Stephanie had told them about Sarah and her shawl was making her imagine things.

She blinked, and when she opened her eyes again, the thing had disappeared. *It was definitely my imagination,* she decided.

Mary Beth finished sealing her letter and carried her desk chair back to her corner of the room. Then she stuck the letter under her pillow, hopped into bed, and pulled her tattered quilt to her chin.

That was better. Old Raggedy would chase away any ghosts. If Andie and Jina knew she slept with a "blankie," they'd probably laugh. But she didn't care what her roommates thought.

She crinkled the threadbare fabric of the quilt between her fingers. It smelled like her room at home—a mixture of rabbit fur, doggie breath, and flowers. Mary Beth inhaled deeply, rolled onto her side, and fell asleep.

"Look, if mornings are going to go smoothly, we've got to have a system," Andie said bossily from her bed. "Red? Are you awake?"

Mary Beth squeezed her eyes tight shut. It was only seven in the morning. There was no way she wanted to hear about Andie's system.

"I'll use the bathroom first," Andie continued. "While I'm showering, one of you can brush your teeth or whatever."

"Oh, stuff it, Andie," Mary Beth heard Lauren say. "Whoever gets up first should get the shower."

"I don't have an eight o'clock class, so I don't care," Jina mumbled from under her covers.

"What do you think, Mary Beth?" Lauren asked.

"Your idea is great, Lauren. Whoever gets up first gets the shower—and all the hot water." Springing up from bed, Mary Beth grabbed her shower bucket and sprinted into the bathroom.

Andie flew after her, but she was too late. With a triumphant grin Mary Beth slammed the door in her face and locked it. A few minutes later she turned on the shower. The hot water felt great when she stepped in.

As she shampooed her hair, she thought excitedly about her schedule of classes: math, English, earth science, lunch. Then she had study skills, American history, and literature. She thought back to the letter she'd written to her parents. Maybe she shouldn't send it after all. She'd only been at Foxhall one day. Things were bound to get better.

"Hey, Freckle-face! Did you drown in there?" Andie pounded on the door, then rattled the knob.

Maybe they wouldn't get better.

"I'll be out in a minute," Mary Beth called back as she rinsed her hair. She was just turning off the water when the door swung open. Andie stood in the doorway, grinning at her.

Mary Beth grabbed her towel off the rack

and wrapped it around her. "How'd you get in?"

Andie held up a straightened paper clip. "Piece of cake. So hustle out of here."

Embarrassed to be wearing nothing but a towel, Mary Beth picked up her shower bucket and hurried out of the bathroom. Lauren and Jina stared at her as she stood in the middle of the room, dripping all over the linoleum.

Jina was sitting on the edge of her bed, bent over, tying her tennis shoes. Her straight black hair was pulled back in a stubby pony-tail.

Lauren was dressed in leggings and a baggy T-shirt. She'd been brushing her hair, but now the brush hovered above her head.

Clutching the towel tight to her, Mary Beth glanced awkwardly around the room. Where was she supposed to get dressed?

"I'll see you at the cafeteria," Lauren said, tossing her brush onto the dresser.

"And I'm going to the barn," Jina said quickly. She jumped up and followed Lauren out the door.

Why are they in such a hurry? Mary Beth wondered. *They probably want to visit the horses before breakfast.* Mary Beth dropped her towel and pulled on khaki pants and a dark green polo shirt. Then she felt around under her pillow until she found the letter she'd written. She'd mail it right after breakfast.

Her hair was still damp when she thumped down the staircase of the dorm and out through the front doors. The campus looked cheery in the bright sun, and a bell was chiming from the tower of the school chapel. All around her students were hurrying to breakfast. With a sinking feeling, Mary Beth remembered that today she was going to have her first riding lesson. *And maybe my last,* she told herself grimly.

Putting that thought straight out of her mind, Mary Beth continued toward the cafeteria.

As she passed the administration building she slowed and looked at the stone arch, remembering the mysterious white figure she'd seen last night. There were no such things as ghosts. So what could it have been?

When she finally reached the cafeteria, Mary Beth threaded her way through the maze of tables to the one where Lauren was sitting. About thirty girls and a half dozen teachers were already eating. Since most of the faculty lived on the school grounds, they often shared meals with the one hundred and eighty students.

Behind Mary Beth, more and more girls continued to pour into the dining room. She put her books on the table, then grabbed a banana and a bagel from the cold food counter. Lauren had toast and orange juice.

"Let me see your schedule," Lauren said when Mary Beth sat down.

Mary Beth pulled a wrinkled slip of paper from her notebook and handed it to her roommate.

"Oh, good. We have history, English, and study skills together," Lauren said. "And riding, of course. But that's not until after three o'clock, when regular classes are all over."

Riding. Mary Beth felt like she'd been punched in the stomach. Slowly she set down her bagel.

"Everyone rides at the same time, even the beginners, unless you're a big-deal rider like Jina and the girls on the riding team," Lauren chattered on. "Last night Jina told me she goes to a special trainer off-campus three afternoons a week. Can you believe it? We won't all be getting the same lessons, though. You might be at one end of the ring and I might be at the other end. But all the beginners have a riding partner to help them the first week."

"A riding partner?" Mary Beth echoed.

Lauren nodded. "You know, someone to teach you how to saddle and bridle a horse, groom it, that kind of stuff. Maybe you'll get me for a partner. Wouldn't that be fun?"

Mary Beth managed a smile. "Sure."

Starting to feel hungry again, she peeled the banana and tried to forget about riding. "That was some wild story Stephanie told us last night about that ghost." Mary Beth leaned forward. "You don't think it could actually be true, do you?"

Lauren shrugged. "It's possible, I guess. I mean, even my mother heard about Sarah when she went to Foxhall ages ago." She eyed Mary Beth. "Why? Did *you* believe it?"

Mary Beth flushed. "No. But last night I..." Her voice trailed off.

Lauren's eyes widened. "You saw the ghost?"

Mary Beth nodded. She told Lauren about the white figure. When she was finished, her roommate slowly let out her breath.

"Wow. Do you think it could have been Sarah Pendleton?"

"Are you guys still talking about that ghost?" a voice from behind them said.

Mary Beth turned. Andie was staring down at them, a stack of books in her arms. "It's none of your business," Mary Beth told her, tossing her ponytail.

Andie dropped her books on the table, then sat down in the chair next to Mary Beth. "You know, Finney, if I were you, I'd be very nice to me," she said in a low voice.

"Why's that?" Mary Beth asked, suddenly feeling nervous.

Andie chuckled. "Guess who's your riding partner this week?"

Mary Beth gulped. "Who?" she practically squeaked.

Andie grinned. "Me!"

Mary Beth's heart clunked straight to her toes. She couldn't believe her lousy luck. Andie Perez was going to be her riding partner!

"How'd *you* get to be Mary Beth's riding partner?" Lauren said, frowning. "And how come you got to ride yesterday too? Are you the teacher's pet already?"

Andie gave her a smug look. "No. Head-monster Frawley has this idea that if I'm kept busy every second of every day, I won't get in trouble. I've been kicked out of three other boarding schools, you know," she added, sounding very proud.

"Gee, what an accomplishment," Mary Beth muttered.

Andie ignored her. "Dad says Foxhall is my last chance. Anyway, Frawley assigned me to be Caufield's slave at the stables." She grinned. "Who cares? I'm going to get kicked out of this school too."

"Why do you want to get kicked out of school?" Lauren asked. "You just got here."

Andie shrugged. "I don't know. I guess because it makes my dad mad."

"Are you wearing those shorts so you'll get in trouble?" Mary Beth asked. "The dress regulations in the Foxhall handbook say you can't wear them to class."

Andie just shrugged.

"Well, so far Mr. Frawley doesn't seem to be noticing," Lauren said. She nodded toward the corner table where the headmaster was sitting with a group of students. He was waving a spoon in the air as he talked.

"Hmmm," Andie said. "I guess I'll just have to do something more dramatic." And standing up, she grabbed her books and marched past Mr. Frawley's table.

Lauren turned to Mary Beth again. "So back to Sarah," Lauren said. "The moon will still be bright tonight, so let's stay up late and watch for her ghost. If we both see it, then we'll know it's real."

Mary Beth nodded. "Sure. If I'm still alive

after my first riding class, anyway. With Andie as a riding partner, I'll probably be the first student in Foxhall history to be stomped to death by a giant horse foot."

"Hoof," Lauren corrected. "But don't worry. It usually only hurts for a little while."

Read ten pages of Hamlet, *the first chapter of earth science, and Chapters One and Two of history. Solve problems 1–25 in math and answer questions A–H in history.*

Mary Beth groaned as she tucked her assignment notebook into her backpack. She couldn't believe all the homework she'd been assigned on her *first* day of classes. No wonder the whole school had mandatory study hall after dinner.

"Hey! Ready to ride?" Lauren jogged up beside her on the courtyard, her shiny hair bouncing behind her in a ponytail.

"Uh, sure," Mary Beth said as she and Lauren headed toward the dorm. "I guess so. What are you so happy about?" Lauren was smiling from ear to ear.

"I'm just excited about riding class!" Lauren said happily. "Today we find out which horse we'll be assigned. I hope I get Whisper."

"I'll keep my fingers crossed for you." Shifting her books to one arm, Mary Beth opened the door to Bracken Hall. Cool, air-conditioned air wrapped around her like a chilled blanket.

"Ahh," she said with a sigh. "I'm never leaving this dorm again."

Lauren leaped up the stairs. "Riding starts at three-thirty, so you have fifteen minutes to change." She stopped on the top step and looked over her shoulder at Mary Beth. "I bet you don't even have any boots."

"Boots?" Mary Beth repeated as she followed Lauren upstairs and into their room. "Can't I just wear tennis shoes?"

Lauren shook her head. "No way. You could get your foot caught in a stirrup and get dragged. I'll lend you a pair of mine."

"Dragged by a horse? Oh, great." Mary Beth threw her books on her desk and flopped backward on the bed. A dark, handsome vampire with two glistening fangs stared back at her.

Mary Beth squealed and jumped off the bed. "Look!" she exclaimed, pointing at the ceiling.

Lauren threw back her head. "Hey, that's a cool Teen Vampire poster."

"I didn't hang that up there. Andie must have."

"That does seem like Andie's idea of a joke." Kneeling down, Lauren began rummaging under her bed. Finally she pulled out a pair of ankle-high, brown leather boots with laces. "These are my paddock boots," she said. "You can wear them until you get a chance to buy some."

"Thanks," Mary Beth said, taking the boots. "But what are you going to wear?"

"My high black boots. They're not real new, so I use them to ride all the time."

Mary Beth pulled jeans from her drawer. Lauren was slipping on skintight black pants.

"What are those?" Mary Beth asked.

"Schooling sweats. Aren't they neat? Everyone's got them."

"Schooling sweats?"

Lauren laughed. "Don't worry. You'll get used to hearing so much horse talk."

I doubt it, Mary Beth thought as she pulled on the paddock boots. They were too small, but they didn't pinch too badly. Then she opened the drawer to her desk and pulled out a pair of scissors.

"I have to do something before we leave,"

she told Lauren. Jumping up on the bed, she carefully peeled the poster from the ceiling.

"What are you planning?" Lauren asked.

Mary Beth grinned. "You'll see."

Ten minutes later they were trudging up the hill to the stables. Lauren was chattering about the horse-show schedule, but Mary Beth was only half-listening. As each step brought her closer to the horses, her insides knotted a little tighter. When they reached the stables, about forty girls were clustered around Mrs. Caufield. Beyond the circle of students Mary Beth could see Jina standing by a stall. She was wearing tan schooling sweats and shiny paddock boots. Superstar's head hung over the bottom door as he looked around curiously. Above the stall was a wood plaque with his name engraved on it in gold.

Mrs. Caufield was looking at a clipboard as she called the roll. When Mary Beth heard her name, she called out "Here!"

And I wish I wasn't, she added to herself.

A few minutes later Andie sidled up to her. She was wearing jeans and high black rubber boots. "So, how'd you like the poster?" she whispered.

"Loved it," Mary Beth whispered back.

"Teen Vampire's my favorite."

Andie snorted. "Sure he is. So, have you seen the horse you've been assigned?"

"No. Is it a nice one?"

"Oh, yeah. A real sweetheart." Andie loomed closer. "Guess what his name is?"

Mary Beth hesitated. "Gentle Ben?"

Andie chuckled. "Not even close. It's—"

"Andie!" Mrs. Caufield's sharp voice cut in. "I'd appreciate it if you would give me your attention."

"Yes, Mrs. Caufield," Andie replied sweetly.

"Lauren Remick?" Mrs. Caufield continued. "This week you'll be riding Whisper. You'll start lessons with the dressage instructor, Katherine Parks."

Lauren squealed with delight.

"Mary Beth Finney?"

"Yes!" Mary Beth raised her hand.

"Welcome to the riding program." Mrs. Caufield smiled. "Foxhall embraces beginners as well as expert riders. To help you get off to a good start, you'll be partnered with Andrea Perez for the week. Since you two are roommates, I thought it would be a nice way for you to get to know each other better."

Andie slapped a hand over her mouth,

trying hard to stifle her laughter.

"Andie!"

Andie snapped to attention. "Yes!"

"Introduce Mary Beth to her horse and show her how to groom him."

"Yes, Mrs. Caufield," Andie replied seriously. She turned to Mary Beth as the riding director continued with the roll. "I'll be happy to introduce you two," she said. "Right this way."

Mary Beth followed Andie toward one of the stalls. *Let my horse be little and sweet*, she thought as she twisted her hands together nervously. *Let him be little and—*

"Over here," Andie's voice cut in. She was standing next to the stall at the farthest end of the stable. A horse the size of an elephant was hanging its head over the door. "Mary Beth Finney," Andie said, "meet Dangerous Dan."

Dangerous Dan!

"Excuse me," Mary Beth croaked. Clutching her stomach, she stumbled off down the aisle. She made it around to the back of the stable before throwing up in the grass.

"Something you ate?" Andie asked from behind her.

"Leave me alone," Mary Beth said. Why was this girl always picking on her?

Andie handed her an open soda bottle. Mary Beth eyed it suspiciously.

"Hey, it's not poisoned or anything."

Mary Beth took a sip and the soda fizzed up her nose, making her cough.

Andie crossed her arms. "You really are scared of horses, aren't you?"

"Only when their first name is Dangerous,"

Mary Beth said. She took another sip of soda, then handed the bottle back to Andie. "Okay. I'm ready." She took a deep breath. "Get me a stepladder and show me how to brush that thing."

"That *thing* is named Dan. But don't worry; he really is gentle. His name's a joke. Mrs. Caufield wouldn't assign a mean horse to a beginner."

"That's comforting," Mary Beth murmured as she strode back down the aisle to Dan's stall. But when he stuck his head over the door, she jerked back.

"Why is he so *big*?"

"He's part Clydesdale," Andie explained. "That's a breed of draft horse."

Mary Beth gave her a blank look.

Andie sighed. "You know. Those big horses that pull the wagon in the beer commercials on TV?"

"Oh. Right." Mary Beth studied Dan. His head was about two feet long, with a wide white blaze down the middle. He was chestnut, like Whisper, but his mane was blond, and he seemed twice as big. *Which means his teeth are probably twice as big*, Mary Beth told herself as she squinted up at the horse's mouth. He was chewing a hunk of hay, and his teeth and jaws were making a thunking sound—like he was grinding up someone's bones.

"I can see why a horse like Dan would be good for pulling a wagon," Mary Beth said. "But why would anyone want to ride him? I mean, if you fell off, it would take an hour before you hit the ground."

"So don't fall off," Andie said with a shrug. Picking up a wooden box with a handle, she unlatched the stall door. "This is a grooming kit. They're kept in the tack room. Each school horse has his own."

Mary Beth stepped closer and peered inside the stall. "Dan takes up the whole stall! There's no way I can fit in there with him."

"Get real," Andie said. "Only the fancy new barn has crossties, so we have to groom the horses in the stalls."

Grabbing Mary Beth's sleeve, Andie jerked her into the stall. "This is called a dandy brush." She stuck a wooden bristle brush under Mary Beth's nose. "You whisk it along the hair, like this, to get off the dirt and manure."

Andie made a back-and-forth motion on Dan's side. "But be careful not to hit his ticklish spots or he might kick."

"Kick?" Mary Beth croaked.

Thrusting the brush in Mary Beth's hand, Andie pointed to the horse. "Now you do it. I'll be back in a second—I've got to groom Ranger."

"Wait!" Mary Beth yelped as Andie headed out the stall door. "How do I know where his ticklish spots are?"

Andie rolled her eyes. "Don't worry, you'll find out," she said, and shut the half-door.

Mary Beth leaned over the top of the door. "Shouldn't he have a leash on or something?" she called after her roommate.

But Andie kept walking as if she hadn't heard her, then disappeared into another stall.

Mary Beth held her breath. She could hear Dan grinding his teeth as he chewed his hay. Slowly she turned around. The horse was staring at her, his brown eyes placid.

Mary Beth grinned stupidly. "So, hi, Dan, you great big thing. I'm supposed to clean you." She held up the dandy brush. "With this. Only you have to tell me when it tickles. So whinny or something."

Dan reached down to pick up another mouthful of hay. Mary Beth moved a tiny step closer. His side looked like a big hairy wall ending in two hard, sharp feet.

Hooves, Mary Beth corrected herself. She raised the brush and gingerly whisked it down his neck. Ignoring her, Dan continued to eat.

Feeling a bit braver, Mary Beth brushed the huge horse's neck, then whisked off the dirt caked along his side. Standing on tiptoes she tackled his back next, working her way down his tummy to his hind leg. *This isn't so bad*, she thought as the dirt flew off, revealing a shiny red coat.

Suddenly Dan raised his back leg and switched his tail.

Mary Beth jumped for the door. Dan just turned his big head and gazed at her calmly.

Mary Beth's heart pounded. *It's all right*, she told herself. *He's not mad. If I could just do the other side, this grooming stuff would be finished.*

But how was she going to get past Dan's head and big teeth to the other side? And there was no way she was walking behind his rear and his huge feet.

Hooves, Mary Beth corrected herself again. So where was Andie?

She stuck her head over the stall door. Andie was coming up the aisle.

"Good, you're done," Andie said. "Now you have to use the body brush."

Mary Beth backed away as Andie swung open the stall door. "But I'm not done yet. I—"

Andie took a brush with soft bristles and ran it down Dan's neck. "You use the body brush to get down to the skin and make the hair really shine."

Mary Beth nodded.

"At the same time you keep the body brush clean by drawing it across the currycomb," Andie went on. "See?" She held out a blue plastic thing with a handle and ran the bristles of the brush over it. Dust and hair sprayed into the air. Mary Beth sneezed, and Dan stopped chewing to stare at her.

"Start at the horse's poll and work down the neck all the way to his tail," Andy continued. "Be sure you do a good job. Old Caufield's going to inspect him. And if he doesn't look good, it's both our necks."

"But I—" Mary Beth stammered, then her eyelids slammed shut as another sneeze exploded from her mouth. When she opened her eyes, Andie was gone.

Great. Mary Beth looked at the two different brushes in her hands. *I'm supposed to start at the poll. But where is it?*

She still had to do the other side of Dan, too, she reminded herself as she glanced up at the horse. He had backed up slightly. Maybe if she sucked in her stomach, she could inch around his head to his right side.

"Whoa, Danny boy," she crooned as she sidled her way past his big teeth and large, unblinking eyes. When she had safely reached the other side, she breathed a sigh of relief.

Then she realized how dark it was inside the stall. Dan was so big, he blocked out the light from the stall door. And behind her was a wooden wall.

A *high* wooden wall, Mary Beth noticed. If Dan decided to move toward her, there would be nowhere to go.

Suddenly the horse shifted his weight, knocking into her. Mary Beth jumped back, her shoulders hitting the wall with a painful smack. Then he swayed even closer, until his sleek side pinned her against the wall.

Frantically Mary Beth pushed him with both arms. "Move, you oaf!"

Dangerous Dan didn't budge. Tears filled Mary Beth's eyes. There was no way out.

She was going to be squashed like a bug!

Mary Beth squeezed her eyes shut. *This isn't happening,* she told herself. *A giant animal is not going to crush you. It's just one of your nightmares.*

"Mary Beth? Are you in there?" Andie called from the other side of Dan.

"Yes," she gasped. "Hurry."

Andie ducked under Dan's head. "What are you doing?" she asked, straightening up in the narrow space beside the horse's neck.

Mary Beth's mouth dropped open. "What do you mean, what am I doing?" she asked indignantly. "I'm about to be smushed."

Andie gave her a strange look. "Why don't you make him move over?"

Mary Beth flushed. "Well, I—"

"Get over, Dan," Andie told the big horse,

poking her knuckles into his belly. Automatically he swung his hindquarters away from her.

"It's time to parade the horses in front of Caufield," Andie said, holding up a halter.

Mary Beth exhaled with relief.

"Why haven't you finished grooming Dan yet?" Andie asked, frowning. "You've had half an hour." She yanked the brush from Mary Beth's hand and furiously began whisking dirt from Dan's side.

"Inspection!" a voice hollered.

"This will have to do," Andie said. She slid a halter over Dan's head and buckled it. Then she led the horse past Mary Beth and out the stall door.

When Mary Beth joined Andie and Dan, about fifteen other girls were leading their horses into the middle of the courtyard. Lauren and Whisper were already lined up. Whisper's chestnut coat gleamed in the sun. Jina was leading Superstar, his gray coat glistening, out of his stall.

When the horses were all in a row, Mrs. Caufield came out of her office, a clipboard in her hand. Slowly she began to walk down the line of horses.

Mary Beth glanced right, then left. Everyone looked very serious. Everyone's horse was sparkling clean.

Except hers.

It was only the first day of the riding program, and she'd already blown it.

As Mrs. Caufield came down the row, she made notes on her pad. Then she looked up at Dan. Stopping in her tracks, she studied him from all angles. "So, Andie." The riding director raised an eyebrow. "Why isn't your partner's horse properly groomed?"

Mary Beth quickly stepped forward. "It's my fault, Mrs. Caufield. I'm, ummm..." Her face burned. "...A little afraid of horses and—"

"Andie?" Mrs. Caufield's voice was sharp. "Did you show Mary Beth how to brush the mane and pick out the hooves? Or were you too busy running back and forth to Ranger's stall?"

Andie lowered her eyes. "I was too busy running back and forth to Ranger's stall."

"That's what I thought. Tomorrow I want you to spend every minute with Mary Beth. I want her horse to shine."

"Yes, Mrs. Caufield."

When the riding director moved on to the next horse, Mary Beth's gaze darted to Andie. Her roommate's brow was furrowed as she clucked to Dan and led him back to his stall.

Mary Beth hesitated, then followed them.

The stall door slammed in her face. "I'm sorry you got in trouble," Mary Beth said.

Silently Andie unbuckled the halter. "It wasn't your fault," she replied tersely. "And thanks for trying to take the rap."

"All beginners in the office for a lesson on tack!" Mrs. Caufield called. "All riders saddle up and go to the outdoor ring with Kathy."

"See you later, Andie," Mary Beth said. She ran her hand down Dan's nose. It really was velvety soft. And he hadn't tried to hurt her.

Tomorrow she'd try harder.

"See you," Andie said.

"I can't believe it," Mary Beth said with a sigh that night. "I even have riding homework." She was lying on her bed in the suite, holding a piece of paper with a saddle and bridle drawn on it. Who would have thought a saddle had more than fifteen parts to memorize?

Dinner was over, and for the next two hours, from seven to nine, the girls were confined to their rooms for study time.

Leaning against the headboard of her bed, Jina was reading *Island of the Blue Dolphins*. She and Mary Beth were in the same honors literature class.

"Maybe we can do those study questions together," Mary Beth said to her.

Jina checked her watch. "Okay. But at eight forty-five I've got to start on math or I'll never finish." She shook her head. "I don't know how I'm going to do all this work on days when I have lessons in Middlefield."

Lauren was hunched over her desk, an open book in front of her. "Stephanie warned me about how they piled on homework, but I didn't believe her."

"So don't do it," Andie said impatiently. She was lying on her bed, her stockinged feet propped against the wall, filing her nails.

Mary Beth, Jina, and Lauren all turned to stare at her.

"Either you're incredibly smart and don't have to study or you're incredibly crazy," Lauren said.

Mary Beth giggled. "I think we know which one," she said.

"I heard that, Finney." Andie dropped her

legs from the wall and sat up. "And I wouldn't talk about being crazy. Aren't you the dope who thought she was going to get squashed by a horse?"

Lauren and Jina's gaze swung to Mary Beth.

"You thought *Dan* was going to crush you?" Lauren asked. "He's so sweet."

Mary Beth flushed and quickly retreated behind her work sheet.

"Don't you have any homework?" Jina asked Andie.

"Sure. But if I'm going to get kicked out of school, what's the use of doing it?" Andie threw herself back on her pillow, stuck earphones in her ears, and turned on her Walkman.

Lauren, Mary Beth, and Jina exchanged glances. Listening to music during study time was definitely against the Foxhall rules.

Lauren suddenly got up and reached for something under her bed. "Oh, Mary Beth, I almost forgot," she said. "You got a package today." She pulled out a small brown-paper-wrapped box and handed it to Mary Beth.

"It's from my parents," Mary Beth said. "Express Mail. I wonder what it is?" She ripped open the box and a delicious smell filled the room. "My mom's chocolate chip cookies!" she squealed, lifting the lid off the foil-lined shoebox.

"Wow, those smell wonderful," Lauren said, her eyes lighting up.

Andie snorted as she pulled out her earphones. "I can't believe it. Mommy actually baked cookies to send you on the first day of school?"

"You don't want any?" Mary Beth asked, grinning as she held out the box.

"Well." Andie reached out and took a handful of cookies. She stuffed one in her mouth, then stuck her earphones back in her ears.

"Jina? How about you?" Mary Beth asked.

Jina studied the cookies, then shook her head. "Too fattening."

"Looks like you and I will have to polish them off," Lauren said happily.

For the next hour everyone but Andie studied. At nine o'clock Mary Beth closed her book with a tired sigh.

"I'm beat," Jina said. She took her nightshirt out from under her pillow and went into the bathroom.

Lauren crumpled up her third piece of

paper and threw it into the trash can.

"I'll never get this homework finished," she grumbled. "Never in a zillion years."

"Need help?" Mary Beth offered. She walked to the desk and looked over her friend's shoulder.

"No, thanks," Lauren said, quickly folding the piece of paper she'd been working on. "Hey, why don't we go down to the common room and get a soda?"

"Good idea," Mary Beth said, slipping on her plastic sandals.

Andie pulled out her earphones. "Where are you two going?"

"To get a soda," Lauren said, opening the door of the suite.

Andie jumped off the bed. "I'm coming too. It's almost visiting hour, right?"

When they stepped outside, the hall was already bustling with noisy girls. Several girls wearing robes came out of the suite next door, talking excitedly. Andie, Lauren, and Mary Beth followed them down the steps. When they reached the first floor, Lauren scanned the groups of chattering girls in the common room.

"Looking for Stephanie?" Mary Beth asked.

Lauren nodded. "I don't feel quite as homesick when I see her."

"Gee, I thought I was the only one who was homesick," Mary Beth said.

Andie snorted. "You two are such babies," she said as she pushed past them to join some older girls watching TV.

When she was gone, Mary Beth shook her head. "I wonder what her problem is."

Lauren shrugged. "Who knows? Hey, some girls over there are playing Boggle, my favorite game. Let's get our sodas and watch."

An hour later, when Mary Beth and Lauren returned to the suite, Jina had finished showering and was already tucked in bed, reading a book called *Show to Win.*

Andie was nowhere in sight, but Mary Beth could hear loud singing coming from the bathroom.

Suddenly the lights went out and the bedroom door slammed shut. For a second Mary Beth and Lauren stood there in silence.

Finally Lauren whispered, "What's going on? Jina, did you turn out the lights?"

"No," Jina whispered back from her bed.

Then Mary Beth saw it. A huge, white shape, its arms moving like waves, was silhouetted against the closed door.

"Look!" she said, grabbing Lauren's wrist. "It's the ghost of Sarah Pendleton!"

8

Mary Beth, Lauren, and Jina stared in horror at the mysterious white shape. Suddenly the ghost burst into two sets of hysterical giggles.

"Stephanie—you creep!" Lauren cried, rushing toward the white figure. She whipped the sheet off the "ghost" just as Mary Beth flicked on the lights.

"Gotcha again," Lauren's sister crowed. Christina was standing next to her, holding her sides as she laughed.

Lauren playfully punched Stephanie on the arm. "You stinker."

Stephanie chuckled. "You're right, I am. But it's so much fun scaring my little sister and her friends."

"Hey, speaking of ghosts, wait until you guys hear what Mary Beth saw last night," Lauren said eagerly.

Mary Beth gulped. She couldn't believe Lauren was going to tell Stephanie and Christina about the ghost. The older girls would think she was crazy.

"Lauren, I don't—"

"Last night Mary Beth saw Sarah," Lauren said in a dramatic whisper.

"The ghost?" Stephanie's brows shot up. "Sure." She and Christina both laughed.

"It's true." Lauren went over and turned off the light.

"Hey!" Jina protested from her bed. "I'm trying to read."

Lauren beckoned for her sister to come closer to the window. "You may think Mary Beth's kidding, but I bet she really saw Sarah."

"Oh, come off it," Stephanie said, but she and Christina walked over to the window and looked outside. Mary Beth joined them. Even Jina climbed out of bed to look over their shoulders.

"Well, it probably wasn't a real ghost," Mary Beth said. But when no one scoffed, she added, "It sure looked like one, though. It was right there under the stone arch. And it was wearing something long and white."

"Sounds like our story must have really spooked you," Stephanie said, turning away from the window.

Jina yawned, then shook her head. "This ghost stuff is too strange for me. Besides, I've got to get up early and check on Superstar." She trudged back to bed.

Suddenly the room brightened as the bathroom door swung open.

"Hey! Who turned out the lights?" Andie demanded. She stood in the doorway, wrapped in a towel. "What are you guys doing, anyway?"

"Looking for a ghost," Stephanie told her, grinning.

"Okay, so maybe you don't believe us," Lauren said. She glanced from Jina to Andie to the older girls. "But tonight Mary Beth and I are going to watch for Sarah, and when we see her, we're going to show you all."

Andie snorted. "Well, if you two ghost-busters have any luck, be sure to wake me up."

Stephanie turned to leave. "Come get us too," she said seriously. But as Stephanie went out the door, she and Christina started laughing again.

When they were gone, Mary Beth glared daggers at Lauren. The two older girls would probably tell everyone about Mary Beth Finney seeing a ghost. By tomorrow the whole school would think she was crazy.

"I get the bathroom first," Lauren said quickly. Grabbing her nightgown, she dashed into the bathroom and shut the door.

With a sigh, Mary Beth sat and kicked off her flip-flops. Andie was pulling a tight sleeveless T-shirt over her head. HOT MAMA was written across the front of it.

"Well, it's been a long day and I need my beauty sleep," Andie said, pulling down the bedspread. Mary Beth froze when she suddenly remembered what she'd done that afternoon to get even with Andie for the vampire poster.

With a squeal of surprise Andie jumped backward.

Ha! Mary Beth thought triumphantly. The Teen Vampire was lying in Andie's bed, his head on her pillow. And Andie had definitely been scared.

Spinning around, Andie took a step toward Mary Beth. "You've done it this time, Red," she declared, raising her fists.

Mary Beth felt the blood rush from her

face. The last thing she wanted was to get in a fight with Andie over a stupid poster.

"It was only a joke," she stammered.

"Gotcha!" Andie dropped her fists and started to laugh. "Stephanie's not the only one who can fool you. You thought I was going to hit you, didn't you?"

"Yes, I did," Mary Beth said. Embarrassed, she glanced over at Jina. She was ignoring them, pretending to be asleep.

"Actually, that was pretty funny," Andie said as she slid the poster out from under the spread. Carefully she arranged it so it looked like the Teen Vampire was sitting up in her bed.

"Yeah, I thought so too," Mary Beth said, yawning. She was beginning to feel very tired. She rummaged through her drawer, looking for the T-shirt she'd worn last night. It wasn't there.

With a sigh, she checked in the wardrobe. Sure enough, her T-shirt was balled up in a dusty corner.

Mary Beth pulled it out, then looked around for somewhere to stash her dirty clothes. She was used to her mother washing and folding everything. Finally she settled on her empty suitcase, which she kept under her bed.

What a drag, she thought as she stuffed her shirt inside it. She'd been here only two days, and already she was sick of sharing a tiny room with three other people. Especially since one was a crazy and another one she couldn't figure out. Was riding all Jina thought about? And Lauren was great, but she was spending forever in the bathroom. If she didn't hurry, it would be after lights out before Mary Beth even got to wash her face.

At least I'll be going home soon, Mary Beth told herself. *I won't have to worry about living with roommates again until I go to college. Or maybe I'll just find a school close to Cedarville.*

Reluctantly Mary Beth pulled her new baby doll pajamas from the dresser drawer. The top had puffy sleeves and bows and was covered with tiny pink ballet slippers. Her mother had bought them with squeals of "Aren't they *adorable!* You just have to have these for school, Bethie."

Oh brother. If she wore these, Andie would never let her forget it.

Slumping onto the bed, Mary Beth suppressed a sob. Tears dribbled down her cheeks. She twisted sideways so Jina and Andie couldn't see her, then wiped her eyes with her pajama top.

Boy, did she ever miss her family.

Mary Beth checked her watch. It was nine-fifty. She had ten minutes before lights out to call her parents. Quickly she pulled a quarter from the pocket of her shorts, raced downstairs to the pay phone in the common room, and dialed with trembling fingers.

"Hello?" her mother answered.

"Mom? Hi. It's Mary Beth."

"Bethie! Jim, pick up the extension," she heard her mother call to her dad.

"Mary Beth!" her father's voice boomed a second later. "How are you doing, honey?"

"Fine. Just fine," Mary Beth said. Then her voice broke and she started to cry. "No, I'm not doing fine. I wrote you a letter. I want to come home!"

"Oh, Mary Beth," her mother said, sounding worried. "Are you really that unhappy?"

Mary Beth wiped her sleeve across her eyes. "No. I'm not. It's just that all the girls here are hotshot riders and I miss everyone and—"

"We miss you too, honey," her dad said. "Peggy? Maybe boarding school wasn't such a good idea."

"Now, Jim. She needs to give Foxhall at least a week," her mom said as if Mary Beth wasn't on the other end of the phone. "She wanted to go so badly, remember? But we'll send you a train ticket anyway," she added to Mary Beth. "That way, if things don't work out, you'll already have it. But you call us first."

"Call us anytime, Honeylamb," her father said. "We want to know if you're not happy."

"Thanks, Dad, Mom." Mary Beth sniffled. "And thanks for the cookies." She said good-bye and slowly hung up. Just talking to her parents and knowing it was okay if she went home made her feel better. And maybe things *would* get better at Foxhall and she'd never have to use that ticket. *Maybe*.

"Okay, Mary Beth, now pay attention," Andie said. "Remember that work sheet with the parts of the saddle on it? Well, here they are on the real thing."

Shoving her hands in her jeans pockets, Mary Beth listened intently as Andie pointed out some of the different parts of the saddle—cantle, skirt, stirrup bar, girth, pommel.

The two of them were standing in the stable's tack room. Across one wall was a row of twelve English saddles on triangular racks. Above the saddles hung an assortment of bridles.

"Got it?" Andie asked.

Mary Beth nodded.

"Good," Andie said as she slid a saddle and its pad off the rack. "Because when I explain how to put the saddle on Dan, you're going to have to know what I'm talking about."

Mary Beth nodded again. Like a robot, she tagged after Andie, who was walking briskly toward Dan's stall. But at least this afternoon the two of them had gotten Dan clean.

As they crossed the courtyard Mary Beth waved to Lauren, who was getting on Whisper. With a big grin Lauren waved back.

Mary Beth suppressed a giggle. Their big night watching for Sarah, the ghost, had been a disaster. Both of them had fallen asleep curled up at the end of Lauren's bed near the window.

So much for ghostbusting.

Mary Beth stopped for a moment and glanced around. She didn't see Jina and Superstar anywhere. It was probably one of the afternoons Jina went to her private lesson.

"Are you coming or what?" Andie called. She was hanging over the stall door, frowning impatiently.

In a way, Mary Beth felt sorry for Andie. She probably hadn't wanted to be her riding partner either. There were two other beginning riders in the riding program, but neither one seemed to be afraid of horses.

Heidi Olson was a junior and new at the school. Even though she'd had only a few riding lessons over the summer, she already looked like a natural. Shandra Thomas was a sixth grader, like Mary Beth. She'd never been on a horse either, but unlike Mary Beth, she didn't seem in the least worried.

When Mary Beth finally reached the stall, Dan was already bridled. Eyes closed, lips slack, he looked as if he were going to sleep through the whole lesson.

"I'm only going to explain this once," Andie said as she plucked the saddle from its perch on the door. "You pick up the saddle with the pommel in your left hand and the cantle in your right. Place it on the horse's withers—that's here." Lifting the saddle high, she placed it on Dan's back, right behind his neck.

"You have to run your hands under the saddle pad to make sure it's not wrinkled and Dan's hair is flat and smooth," Andie went on. "Then you go to the horse's off side—that's the right side—to check that the girth isn't twisted."

Mary Beth held her breath as she followed Andie, who had just ducked under Dan's neck. Even though he looked as if he were sleeping, she still didn't trust him and his big teeth. What if he was dreaming about a field of clover and reached to take a bite?

"Girth's fine, saddle pad's smooth," Andie said, moving quickly back to the left side.

This time when Mary Beth scurried under Dan's neck, he flapped his lips sleepily, missing her by an inch. Mary Beth congratulated herself for not flinching.

Andie bent down and grabbed the girth, which was dangling under the horse's belly. "Lift up the saddle flap and buckle it on the girth straps. Got it?"

Mary Beth nodded for the tenth time, though she wasn't sure she'd gotten it at all.

"Tighten it enough to keep the saddle from slipping back, but not so tight that you cut off the horse's wind," Andie went on. "And be sure there's no skin pinched behind the elbows."

Elbows? Frowning, Mary Beth studied Dan's leg. She couldn't find anything that looked like a horse elbow.

"Beginners! Bring your horses to the courtyard for mounting instructions!" Mrs. Caufield said as she walked quickly past the stalls.

"That's me, right?" Mary Beth said, surprised.

"Right." Pushing open the stall door, Andie clucked to Dan and led him out.

"Does this mean I have to get on a horse?" Mary Beth asked as she jogged after Andie.

"Yeah, you have to get on a horse. This is the *riding* program, remember?" She chuckled. "But hey, don't worry. I'll help you."

Mary Beth wrinkled her nose. She didn't know if that should make her feel better or worse.

Andie halted Dan in the middle of the courtyard next to two other horses. Quickly Mary Beth scanned Heidi and Shandra's faces. They both looked so excited.

"You're just getting *on* and *off*," Andie whispered. "It's not like Caufield expects you to gallop away."

"Right." Mary Beth nodded. "Just on and off."

"All right, beginners, listen up," Mrs. Caufield said. "First I want you all to gather around Andie. She's going to demonstrate how to mount."

The other horses and riders crowded closer to Andie and Dan.

"There are two correct ways to mount a tall horse," Mrs. Caufield continued. "One, you lower the stirrup so you can get your foot in it. Or two, you can have someone give you a leg up. Today we will practice the first method. Ready, Andie?"

With a nod, Andie checked the girth, then lengthened the stirrup. Putting the reins in her left hand, she stood with her left shoulder against Dan's and stuck the toe of her left boot in the stirrup. Then she pivoted to face the horse's side. Next she put her left hand on Dan's neck and her right hand on the cantle and with a light bounce pulled herself up. Finally she swung her right leg over the cantle and settled in the saddle.

When Andie was safely on Dan, Mary Beth exhaled. She hadn't realized she'd been holding her breath.

"Good job, Andie," Mrs. Caufield said. "Girls, I want you to note several things Andie did that are so important." She looked around at the beginning riders to make sure they were paying attention.

"First, she checked her girth before getting on. Second, she held the reins taut so the horse couldn't pull his head down to eat or walk off. Third, she—"

Check your girth, hold the reins tight. Mary Beth mentally ticked off the list. *Put your left foot in the stirrup, no your right, no your left.*

She groaned silently in frustration. Her head was spinning. Now she had no idea how Andie had gotten on Dan.

"Okay, riding partners, help your riders to mount," Mrs. Caufield said finally.

Mary Beth's heart pounded as Andie dismounted effortlessly.

"Hey, Red, don't panic. I'll get you on," Andie said.

Numb with fear, Mary Beth nodded. Andie's voice was calm as she told her what to do.

"Right toe in the stirrup, grab hold of the saddle, now swing the left leg over."

Mary Beth followed her roommate's instructions obediently. When she lifted herself up in the stirrup, she shut her eyes tight. Higher and higher she flew as she struggled up and into the saddle.

To Mary Beth's relief, Dan didn't move. As soon as she felt her backside hit the leather seat, she opened her eyes—and gasped.

She was so high up, her head seemed to be

in the clouds. Suddenly terror gripped her insides. Something was wrong. Where was the pommel? Where was Dan's head?

Then it hit her. She was facing Dan's tail. She'd mounted her horse backward!

10

Loud laughter exploded below Mary Beth's right foot. She looked down. Andie was doubled over, laughing hysterically.

"You made me get on backward on purpose!" Mary Beth said angrily. Then Dan stomped his foot, throwing her forward.

She grabbed the back of the saddle with both hands. Beside her the other riders and their partners had started laughing.

"Andie, what is going on here?" Mrs. Caufield strode over to them, hiding a grin behind the clipboard.

Andie shrugged and smiled innocently. "I told Mary Beth how to mount, but I guess she was so scared she got mixed up."

"I did *not* get mixed up," Mary Beth sputtered through clenched teeth. "And I wasn't scared, either," she added, glaring at Andie.

Mrs. Caufield looked up and touched Mary Beth's ankle reassuringly. "There's nothing to be afraid of," she said. "To dismount, swing your left leg slowly back over Dan's neck. I'll be here in case you fall."

In case you fall! The words screamed in Mary Beth's head. But she didn't dare say anything. She already looked like the stupidest person on earth.

Taking a deep breath, she tried to follow the director's instructions, but her hands and legs felt like lead weights. Tipping forward, she swung her left leg behind her. Halfway over, her knee stuck on Dan's neck.

Andie snorted with laughter.

"Keep your right hand on the back of the saddle," the director continued. "At the same time, twist your body to the left. Then put your left hand on the pommel and kick your leg free."

Mary Beth frowned in concentration. On the count of three, she jerked her leg across Dan's shaggy mane. Suddenly he shifted his weight, and Mary Beth lost her grip on the saddle.

With a cry she fell backward, right on top of

Mrs. Caufield. The director caught her by the shoulders, breaking her fall. Then the two of them tumbled to the ground.

Mary Beth scrambled to her feet.

"I'm so sorry," she apologized, her cheeks flaming.

Mrs. Caufield gave an exasperated sigh. Andie jumped to the director's side, her hand outstretched to help her up.

"Don't worry about it," Mrs. Caufield said when she got to her feet. "You aren't the first beginner to get on a horse backward."

Mary Beth looked at the ground.

"Though you *are* the first to fall on top of me," the director added. Brushing off her jeans, she walked away to help another rider.

Andie snickered. "Boy, you're in trouble now."

Mary Beth turned on her. "No, *you're* in trouble," she said, poking her finger in her roommate's chest. "I don't want you for my partner anymore."

For a second, Andie looked surprised. Then her smug expression returned. "So who else is going to help you?" she asked, tossing her mane of hair behind her shoulders.

"I'll just have to learn on my own," Mary

Beth retorted. Yanking Dan's reins from Andie's grasp, she led him back to the stall.

That night after lights out Mary Beth pulled a flashlight from under her pillow. For a second she listened to Lauren and Jina's hushed breathing and Andie's erratic mumbling.

They were all asleep.

Flicking on the flashlight, she aimed the beam at page seven of *The Manual of Horsemanship*, the textbook required for her riding class. The first chapter was called "The Rider— Mounting and Dismounting." Quickly she read through, memorizing everything. Then she flipped to the section on saddlery.

Mary Beth grimaced when she saw that it was sixty-eight pages. But she told herself that she could learn it. She *had* to learn it.

That afternoon when she'd complained to Mrs. Caufield about Andie, the director had stood firm about the two girls remaining partners. That meant Mary Beth had to make sure Andie could never make a fool of her again.

Tomorrow they were practicing mounting and dismounting and bridling a horse. Mary Beth turned to the heading "Putting On and Fitting a Bridle." The page showed a picture of a girl sticking her fingers in a horse's mouth.

Mary Beth began to feel nauseous. Maybe this wasn't going to work after all.

Suddenly a clunking sound against the windowpane startled her from her thoughts. Slowly she shut her book, climbed out of bed, and tiptoed to the window.

The moon was full, and a strong wind whipped the tops of the trees. *Crack!* A flying branch hit the glass. Mary Beth jerked back. Then a flash of light caught her eye. A white figure was gliding across the courtyard, her gown flapping around her legs.

Sarah!

Spinning from the window, Mary Beth ran over to Lauren's bed.

"Lauren, wake up." She shook her roommate's shoulder.

Lauren threw her hand over her eyes, then peeked through her fingers. "Is it time to get up already?" she mumbled sleepily.

"No. It's the ghost!"

Lauren sat bolt upright. "The ghost?"

"Floating across the courtyard!"

"This is great!" Lauren whispered excitedly. "I've got to see her!" Throwing back the covers, she leaped out of bed and ran with

Mary Beth to the window.

The two of them pressed their noses to the glass, their breath making frosty clouds.

"I don't see her," Lauren said in a hushed voice.

"Me neither. Wait! Look under the trees." Mary Beth pointed to a flicker of white. Only the blowing leaves cast such eerie shadows, she wasn't sure there was a ghost at all.

"It has to be her!" Lauren whispered.

"Who's her?" a sleepy voice asked behind them.

When Mary Beth and Lauren spun around, Jina was peering over their shoulders. Her golden eyes were half-open, and she gave a huge yawn.

At the same time Andie bolted upright. Her hair was sticking out all over her head, making her look like a startled lion.

"What's going on?" she asked, glancing around suspiciously.

"It's the ghost," Mary Beth whispered.

Climbing out of bed, Andie came up beside Jina to look out the window with the rest of them.

"Hey, there really *is* something down there," Jina said.

"I see it too," Andie chimed in.

"Let's go get Christina and your sister," Mary Beth said to Lauren. "This will prove I wasn't seeing things."

"Good idea." Turning, Lauren immediately headed for the door, but Mary Beth caught her arm.

"Bad idea," she said. "Remember the dorm rules? If we get caught prowling in the halls after hours, we'll be in big trouble."

"Not *big* trouble," Andie said. "Just Breakfast Club."

"What's that?" Jina asked, looking puzzled.

Lauren cocked one brow. "Breakfast Club's not so bad. We'd just have to get up early on a Saturday morning and study in the cafeteria."

"Well, count me in." Andie rubbed her hands together gleefully.

"Jina?" Lauren asked.

Jina hesitated. "I don't know. I have to get up so early—"

"Listen to you." Andie folded her arms across her chest. "Will you loosen up a little, rich girl?"

"Oh, all right. I'll go," Jina said finally, to Mary Beth's surprise.

"I'll lead the way," Lauren volunteered.

Slowly she opened the suite door. She peered right, then left, down the hall.

"We'd better hurry," Mary Beth whispered. "Or Sarah will be gone."

Lauren nodded, then sprinted for the stairway. Mary Beth was right on her heels, followed by Jina and a giggling Andie.

But as Lauren turned the corner to go down the stairs, she halted abruptly. Mary Beth skidded into her, almost knocking her down.

Ms. Shiroo, the dorm mother, was coming up the steps, a frown creasing her brow. She wore a silk kimono and had foam rollers stuck in her hair.

And from the look on her face, Mary Beth had a feeling the four of them were in big trouble.

11

"What are you all doing in the hall at one o'clock in the morning?" Ms. Shiroo demanded. Hands on her hips, she glared at the four roommates.

"Uh, um," Lauren stammered. She glanced over her shoulder at Mary Beth.

Mary Beth gulped. "We were—"

"Just helping Lauren get to her sister's room," Andie said smoothly behind her. "The poor girl is sick to her stomach. She threw up twice." She wrinkled her nose as though there were a bad smell back in the suite.

"She said only her sister could make her feel better," Mary Beth added.

Lauren quickly clutched her stomach. "That's right."

"And she was afraid to go down the hall by

herself in the dark," Jina chimed in.

"Right," Lauren repeated.

At first Ms. Shiroo looked unconvinced. Then she sighed. "All right. Lauren, you come with me to see the nurse. Andie, Mary Beth, and Jina, I want you back in bed—on the double. And remember, next time one of you is sick, you come to get me—not a friend or a big sister. Got it?"

All the girls nodded in unison. Ms. Shiroo took Lauren's arm and the two of them went downstairs. Jina led the way back to the room.

"Whew, that was a close one," Mary Beth said, shutting the suite door.

"That was nothing," Andie scoffed as she flung herself onto her bed. "On the trouble scale of one to ten, that was a one. We didn't even get Breakfast Club," she added, sounding disappointed.

"Yeah, well, let's just hope Lauren convinces Shiroo and the nurse she was really sick," Mary Beth said.

Jina yawned. "I don't know about you guys, but I've got a quiz tomorrow and a big horse show Saturday. I'm going back to sleep."

"Me too." Mary Beth started for her bed. Then she changed her mind and went over to the window. The moon had gone under a cloud, and the courtyard was dark. There was no sign of Sarah. But at least this time they had all seen the ghost.

Now her three roommates would know she wasn't crazy.

But who cares what they think? Mary Beth told herself as she crawled back into bed. She was going home soon.

"Lauren! I want to see Whisper more relaxed!" Mrs. Caufield hollered. Lauren was cantering the chestnut horse against the outside rail. "Breathe deep, supple your spine, and slow the tempo."

Lauren nodded. She and Whisper thundered around the ring, the horse's neck arched daintily, her red tail flying behind her.

Mary Beth thought they looked great together. Leaning on the top rail, she and the other two beginners, Heidi and Shandra, watched as the riding director gave a lesson to four of the advanced students.

"'Supple your spine'—it's like listening to a foreign language," Heidi said.

"And I don't think I'll ever learn it," Mary Beth muttered.

Shandra gave her a puzzled look. "Sure you will," she said. Shandra had already passed the tacking up and mounting test.

After studying the riding manual all morning, Mary Beth had thought she was ready too. But now watching Lauren, she felt a little depressed.

Who was she kidding? She'd never win the bet with Andie that she'd be able to post by the end of her first week of riding. Turning her head, she saw Andie leap Ranger over a small practice jump. Andie wasn't as graceful as Lauren, but she had a daring style that made Mary Beth envious.

Even if she stuck with the riding program, she'd never be as good a rider as her roommates.

With a sigh, Mary Beth turned away from the ring and headed for the stable. Dangerous Dan was waiting for her. Earlier, she'd groomed him until he shone. But now came the hard part.

After picking up his bridle and saddle from the tack room, Mary Beth walked heavily to Dan's stall. He greeted her with a mouthful of hay in her face.

"Hey, buddy." She opened the stall door

and watched him munch for a second. She was growing to like the big guy. She'd always loved animals, and despite his name, he was very gentle. Dan turned his head to look at her, then rubbed his cheek on her shoulder.

"Itchy, huh?" Mary Beth scratched his face, then kissed him on the white part of his nose. "You know, Dan, after Saturday I might not be at Foxhall anymore," she told him. Tears pricked her eyes. "I got a train ticket from my parents in the mail this morning. So if things don't work out..." Her voice trailed off. The horse pushed her with his nose, and she stroked his soft neck.

"Let's face it. This whole riding thing has been a joke," Mary Beth went on. "My roommates hate me. Well, at least Andie does. Jina couldn't care less, and Lauren and I are sort of friends, but she's always at the stable, and if I quit riding I'd be—"

She hesitated. Would she really be happy taking dance again?

"I'll be back at Cedarville Elementary with Mrs. Henderson and her hairy chin. Hairier than *yours*," she added.

Lifting his muzzle, Dan chewed loudly in her ear.

"You're tired of listening to this, aren't you?" Mary Beth said. Suddenly she realized that *she* was tired of listening to it too. All she'd been doing was whining lately. When had she turned into such a wimp?

So what if she didn't win the bet with Andie? And so what if she wouldn't ever be as good a rider as her roommates? Foxhall was a beautiful school with great teachers. She even liked the food. Besides, even if she did decide to go back to Cedarville, she needed to prove to herself that she wasn't a scaredy-cat and a quitter.

Picking up the lead line, she hooked it to Dan's halter. Then she took a deep breath. It was time to take her test.

"You bridled and saddled Dan all by yourself?" Andie asked, looking doubtful as she walked around the big horse half an hour later. "And no one helped you get on him?"

Mary Beth nodded. Perched rigidly in the saddle, she didn't dare move or look down.

Andie studied the bridle carefully. "It looks like you got everything adjusted right, too."

"Yes. The egg-butt snaffle is neither too wide nor too narrow for Dan's mouth," Mary

Beth recited from memory, her fingers frozen on the reins. "And the cavesson, or noseband, is halfway between the cheekbones and the mouth."

Andie gave her a funny look. "Has Lauren been helping you? Or did you stay up all night studying?"

Mary Beth just grinned. Dan stomped his hoof, trying to dislodge a fly, and her fingers gripped the reins tighter.

"Hey, looking good," Lauren said as she came up beside Dan, leading Whisper.

"Thanks," Mary Beth replied. "Let's just hope Mrs. Caufield thinks so. She watched me do everything. Now I'm just waiting for my grade."

"Mary Beth!" Mrs. Caufield called. Clipboard in hand, she came up beside the group. "I've given you an *A* on grooming and mounting and an *A* on tacking up, too."

Mary Beth gasped. "Thanks!"

"Tomorrow, Friday, there will be a written test on all you've learned," the riding director continued. "You'll take it first thing, and if you pass it, you're ready to ride."

Ready to ride! Mary Beth's eyes popped open. "I—I'll be ready," she stammered. *I think,* she added silently.

"Good." Mrs. Caufield smiled at her. "You should be very proud of yourself, Mary Beth."

As soon as the director walked away Mary Beth breathed a sigh of relief. Then she leaned forward onto Dan's mane and flung her arms around his neck. "We did it, big guy!"

"Humph." Andie's arms were crossed in front of her as she stared gloomily up at Mary Beth. "I didn't get an *A* on *my* grooming test." Then she grinned. "Congratulations, Red. I didn't think you had it in you."

There was a devilish gleam in her roommate's dark eyes that Mary Beth didn't like. She shifted her weight nervously in the saddle.

"And Dan, old buddy," Andie went on, "you did a good job holding still." She grinned again mischievously. Then, raising her hand, she slapped him soundly on the rump.

Instantly Dan broke into a trot, pitching Mary Beth forward onto his neck. She grabbed his mane as her whole body bounced in the air, and her backside hit the saddle with a painful smack.

"Mary Beth! Pull back on the reins!" Lauren called out from somewhere far away.

Reins. Mary Beth opened her eyes long

enough to see them dangling halfway to the ground. Then she gasped as she realized where Dan was going—his stall!

It flashed through her mind that she'd better do something fast. Dan was so tall that there wasn't room enough for both of them to get through the stall door!

12

"Whoa, Dan!" Lauren yelled. "Pull back on the reins, Mary Beth!"

"Whoa," Mary Beth croaked. Her arms were wrapped around Dan's neck, and her face was buried in his mane.

The reins were dangling two inches from her right hand, but she didn't dare let go of his neck to grab them. *I have to stop him*, she thought frantically. In a few more strides her legs would bash into the sides of the stall door and her head would crack on the top of the doorjamb.

"Dan, whoa!" she hollered finally, loud and firm. The horse's ears flicked back, and he suddenly slowed his stride. Mary Beth couldn't believe he'd actually obeyed her command.

Lauren caught up to them, leading Whisper, at the same time Mary Beth reached for the reins. Straightening, Mary Beth pulled back on the bit while Lauren and Whisper blocked Dan's path from the front.

He halted two feet from the stall door.

"Whew, that was a close one," Lauren gasped.

"Where's Andie?" Mary Beth said furiously. "I'm going to kill her." She swung her right leg over Dan's rump, but in her hurry to get off, her left foot slipped out of the stirrup. Awkwardly she plopped to the ground.

"It's good Caufield didn't see that dismount." Lauren suppressed a giggle. "You would've gotten a D."

"Go ahead and laugh," Mary Beth snapped. "Only I don't think it's so funny."

Lauren looked startled, her smile fading. But then her blue eyes turned stormy. "So you think you're the first person to look stupid on a horse?" she retorted. "I mean, didn't you hear Caufield yelling at me through the whole lesson? Every time I learn something new, I'm a big klutz. And do you know how many times *I've* fallen off?"

Mary Beth raised her eyebrows. "No."

"At least twenty. So what if riding isn't easy

for you? At least you get your homework finished." Tears filled Lauren's eyes as she turned and, clucking to Whisper, stomped off across the courtyard.

Mary Beth's mouth dropped open as she watched her go. *Wow*, she thought. Things weren't so rosy for Lauren either. She'd had no idea her roommate worried so much about riding and homework. What a selfish jerk she'd been.

She glanced around, wondering if everyone else had witnessed Dan running off and Lauren's outburst. But all the girls were busily caring for their horses or chattering among themselves.

Then she caught sight of Jina unloading Superstar from a horse trailer. Both of them looked hot, sweaty, and tired. Mary Beth wondered how Jina managed to fit in the private training with everything Foxhall students were required to do. No wonder she seemed so tense all the time.

And then there was Andie, who had disappeared. *Good*, Mary Beth thought darkly. She never wanted to see that girl again.

But as she led Dan into his stall, it dawned on her that she wasn't really so angry anymore.

One of her worst nightmares—a horse running away with her on him—had just come true, and she'd made it through okay.

Mary Beth smiled in spite of herself.

"Do you need any help with your homework tonight?" Mary Beth asked Lauren as they made their way through the crowded cafeteria to the dinner table.

Setting her tray down beside Jina's, Lauren shook her head. "Thanks anyway. I think I'm catching up. I'll be so glad when Friday night rolls around, though. Just think: two whole days with no homework, no classes, no hot blazers at dinner." Her blue eyes suddenly sparkled. "Hey, they're showing a movie in the auditorium on Saturday. Do you guys want to go?"

Jina shook her head. "I won't be back from the horse show until late," she said.

"I'll go." *If I'm still here, anyway*, Mary Beth added to herself. She'd tucked the train ticket under her pillow, just in case.

Slowly she sat down and smoothed her linen napkin on her lap. Tonight Mr. Frawley was guest faculty member at their table, so she'd have to watch her manners. Two older students were sitting with them too.

"Good evening, girls," Mr. Frawley greeted everyone as he set his tray of food next to Mary Beth's.

"Hey, Mr. F.!" Andie said, coming up behind him. Her tray was piled high with food. She was wearing a bright orange vest under her blazer. "What an honor to eat with you."

Raising one brow, the headmaster turned to look at her. "It's nice to eat with you too, Andrea." With a smile he sat down and spread his napkin carefully on his lap.

Mary Beth held her breath. Andie's dark eyes had that same devilish gleam in them that they'd had before she slapped Dangerous Dan on the rump. Her roommate was definitely up to something.

Mary Beth elbowed Lauren and nodded toward Andie, who was still behind Mr. Frawley. The next instant Andie seemed to trip over a chair leg. "Oops!" she cried, falling forward.

Plates and food flew into the air. Roast beef, mashed potatoes, gravy, and peas landed with a squishy splat onto Mr. Frawley's back and shoulders.

Sputtering angrily, the headmaster leaped up.

"Andrea Perez," he thundered. "You did that on purpose!"

Andie's mouth dropped open in shocked innocence. "How could you say such a thing, Mr. Frawley? It was an accident!" she said, but the smirk on her face gave her away.

Mr. Frawley's face turned nearly as red as the handkerchief he pulled from his sport coat pocket. Several teachers and students rushed forward to help wipe off the dripping food. He waved them away.

Then he turned to the table of girls, who were staring at him silently. "Excuse me, ladies. I will rejoin you after I change. Andrea?" His voice was sharp as he handed her his napkin. "Enjoy cleaning up your dinner. I will see you first thing tomorrow morning."

"Yes, sir!" Andie saluted. As soon as the headmaster left, she whipped around, a gleeful expression on her face.

"I did it! I finally did it! Frawley's going to kick me out of Foxhall for sure," she announced to Lauren, Jina, and Mary Beth. Then, twirling in little circles, she danced her way to the kitchen.

"She is one messed-up person," Lauren said, shaking her head.

Mary Beth picked up her fork and started eating. "You can say that again. Can you imagine spilling food on Frawley on *purpose*? And that sure was a stupid stunt she pulled this afternoon."

"What happened?" Jina asked.

Mary Beth told her about Andie slapping Dan on the rump. Then she glanced over at Lauren. "You know, I'm sorry I yelled at you. It wasn't your fault."

"I know." Lauren grinned. "You were just mad at Andie. But don't feel too bad about her. She's pretty mean to everyone."

"Why is she such a jerk?" Mary Beth asked. "I've never known a girl like her."

"Stephanie told me that Andie's parents got divorced several years ago, and her mom ran off to Europe," Lauren said. "Andie lives with her dad, who's some hotshot businessman and doesn't pay any attention to her at all."

"How does Stephanie know all that?" Jina asked.

Lauren shrugged. "She hears everything."

"Oh," Jina muttered. "That's too bad about Andie's parents." She looked down at her plate of food and quickly started eating.

Lauren turned to Mary Beth. "Speaking of

Stephanie, she was pretty mad that she didn't get to see Sarah last night. Her room's on the other side of the dorm, so tonight she and Christina are sneaking up to our suite to watch."

"Does that mean they believe us?" Mary Beth asked.

"No. But they will," Lauren said. "'Cause I just know that we're going to see Sarah again tonight!"

13

Later that night Mary Beth, Lauren, Christina, and Stephanie were huddled around the window in suite 4B, staring into the courtyard.

"I know she's going to appear; I can just feel it," Lauren whispered.

Stephanie and Christina glanced at each other and giggled.

"You're really into this, aren't you, Lauren?" Christina said.

"Hey, I saw it yesterday too. Whatever it was," Andie said from her bed. She was noisily eating a bag of potato chips. "So don't forget to holler if you do see old Sarah again."

"Even Jina said to wake her up," Lauren reminded Mary Beth.

Mary Beth nodded, her gaze still glued to the grassy courtyard outside the window. The last time she'd spotted the white figure, it had been drifting across the grass as if it had come from their dorm.

"Stephanie, how old is this dorm?" Mary Beth asked.

Stephanie shrugged. "From the way the plumbing works, I'd say about a million years old," she joked. "Actually, it probably dates back to the late 1800s, when the school first opened. Of course, the building's been fixed up since then. Not much, though."

"You mean, this could have been the dorm where Sarah lived?" Mary Beth asked, her eyes widening.

"I guess so."

Lauren glanced around nervously. "I wonder what room she was in."

"I think it was suite 4B," Christina teased.

Mary Beth knew that the older girl was kidding, but goose bumps still prickled up her arms. Then the creak of a door hinge made them all jump. The sound had come from the hallway.

"Someone's out there!" Lauren hissed, grabbing Mary Beth's arm.

"Where? Who?" Andie bolted out of bed.

"Shhh!" Stephanie waved frantically.

Everyone stayed quiet. For a few seconds all Mary Beth heard was Jina's soft breathing. Then there was another creak, and the faint sound of someone walking down the hall.

"She's out there!" Mary Beth squeaked.

"It's probably just another student sneaking down the hall," Christina said.

Andie clapped her hands. "Let's go find out."

"Wait!" Stephanie held Andie back. "Mary Beth, wake up Jina. Then everyone settle down." She pulled a camera with a built-in flash from her bathrobe pocket. "If it *is* Sarah, I don't want you guys scaring her off. This might get us on one of those true-life TV shows."

Mary Beth padded silently across the floor to Jina's bed. "Jina, wake up," she whispered. "Sarah's here."

Jina's eyes flew open. "Here?"

"We think she's out in the hall." Mary Beth nodded toward the closed door. Christina, Andie, and Lauren had their ears pressed against it, listening, while Stephanie fiddled with her camera.

Jina slid out from under the covers. When they were all together, Christina carefully opened the door. Six heads peered into the hallway.

It was empty.

"Where do you think she went?" Lauren asked in a hushed voice.

"I don't know. But if we go looking for her, Shiroo will probably hear us. And if she does, we're cooked," Stephanie said.

Then a loud clunk from below made Mary Beth realize that the person had gone downstairs and she'd opened the big, heavy door to the outside.

"She's going outside!" Mary Beth called out. Forgetting all about Ms. Shiroo, she sprinted from the suite. Behind her five pairs of bare feet padded down the hall and then the steps. By the time they reached the first floor, Mary Beth's heart was racing.

The dorm door was wide open!

"They don't lock it?" Lauren exclaimed.

"Can't," Stephanie replied as she dashed outside. "Fire code or something."

All six girls stopped short on the stone walk and looked around.

"Well, whatever it was, it vanished!" Andie said.

"Look over there!" Mary Beth pointed to

the administration building. A white figure was just coming out of the shadows of the trees and heading for the stone arch. Even though she was pretty scared, Mary Beth felt a little bit relieved. At least Stephanie and Christina would finally get to see the ghost. "Wow. It really does look like a ghost!" Stephanie whispered.

"See? We told you," Lauren said.

Christina started forward. "There's no such thing as ghosts," she said, frowning. "Come on. Let's get a closer look."

Nightshirts and robes flapping in the cool air, the girls moved cautiously across the dewy grass. Mary Beth stopped when she reached the corner of the administration building.

The figure was on the other side of the arch. Mary Beth could see it was definitely a girl about their age. Her long, curly hair was blowing gently in the breeze and her white nightgown billowed around her legs. In the moonlight the girl's bare arms looked luminescent, and her wide eyes seemed to be staring right at Mary Beth.

For a second no one said a word. Then Stephanie whipped her camera out from her pocket and rapidly began snapping pictures of the silent, swaying figure.

"I can't believe it," she muttered with every click.

Mary Beth gulped. Lauren was gripping the hem of her long T-shirt. Behind her she could hear Andie and Jina's ragged breathing.

"You know, I don't really believe in ghosts," Christina whispered. "But that sure looks like one to me."

"Do you think it's Sarah?" Lauren asked.

Mary Beth nodded. "It has to be. And I bet she's looking for whoever killed her."

"Or maybe she's just hunting for her shawl," Jina said, her voice hushed. "Remember the story?"

"Wait a second," Andie suddenly blurted. Pushing between Lauren and Mary Beth, she pointed at the white figure. "That's not a ghost. That's Ellie Martin, one of the girls in the suite down the hall."

Stephanie lowered her camera. "Ellie?"

All six girls stared at the ghostly figure. She was staring back at them, a blank expression in her eyes.

"I should have known," Christina murmured under her breath.

"If she's a real person, then why is she looking at us like that?" Lauren asked.

Mary Beth shook her head. "I don't know. It's pretty weird, though."

"Maybe she's a zombie," Andie suggested.

"A zombie!" Lauren squealed.

"She could be sleepwalking," Stephanie said slowly. "I read about it in my psychology class. Sometimes it happens to kids when they're under a lot of stress."

Andie snorted. "Coming to this crummy school would stress out anybody."

"So what should we do?" Jina asked.

"Well, I do remember reading that you shouldn't wake a sleepwalker up," Stephanie said.

Mary Beth frowned. "If Ellie is the ghost I thought I saw, then she's been walking around outside the last two nights without anyone knowing."

"It's possible," Christina said. "We're all in our rooms with the doors shut."

"Hey!" Lauren snapped her fingers. "Last night Ms. Shiroo said that a noise in the hall woke her up. That's when she came upstairs and found us. But maybe what she really heard was Ellie leaving the dorm."

"Well, if Ellie *is* sleepwalking, then we'd better hurry and get Ms. Shiroo," Mary Beth said. "Before she runs into something or hurts herself."

No one moved.

"Then Shiroo will know we were wandering around out here," Christina pointed out. "And I for one don't want to start out the school year by getting in trouble."

Lauren nodded. "And Shiroo already caught us last night," she reminded her roommates. "So this time we'll be in even bigger trouble."

"Right." Stephanie stuck her camera in her robe pocket and turned to face the others. "Christina and I can't afford to get in trouble, either. You sixth graders won't get anything worse than Breakfast Club, so you guys figure out what to do." With a wave, she and her roommate jogged back to the dorm.

Shocked, Mary Beth watched Stephanie and Christina cross the courtyard. *What wimps!* she thought. And didn't they even care about what might happen to poor Ellie?

Andie broke the silence. "Christina and your sister are real pals," she said.

Lauren shrugged. "This year Steph's trying to win Foxhall's Student Trustee Award or something, so she wants a perfect record."

"Well, we can't just abandon Ellie," Jina said.

"She must have found her way back to her suite before," Lauren pointed out. "Or someone else would have discovered she was sleep-walking."

"Look, guys." Andie turned to face the others. "Go back to the room. I'll run in and tell Shiroo about Ellie. I'll make up some story. Then at least you three won't have to do Breakfast Club."

"You'd do that for us?" Mary Beth asked, surprised.

Andie grinned. "Sure. We're roomies, right? We've gotta help each other out. Besides," she added, "when Frawley gets done with me tomorrow morning, I'm history anyway."

Mary Beth glanced from Lauren to Jina then back to Andie. What should they do? Ellie was still standing in the same position. But now her eyelids had started to droop and her body was beginning to slump.

We can't just leave her here, Mary Beth decided. And she wouldn't feel right if she let Andie take the rap alone.

"No. I'll go with you to tell Shiroo," Mary

Beth said finally. "Breakfast Club can't be that bad. Besides, I might not be here after tomorrow either."

"Why not?" Lauren asked.

"Well, um." Mary Beth felt her cheeks flush in the darkness. "It's not important," she said quickly. "Come on, Andie, let's get Ms. Shiroo before Ellie drops to the ground. Lauren, you and Jina go on back to the suite. There's no sense in all of us getting in trouble."

"No way," Lauren said firmly. "We're all in this together. Jina and I will stay here with Ellie and keep an eye on her. Right, Jina?"

"Right," Jina agreed, sounding a bit reluctant.

"All right! Give me five, guys," Andie said, putting up her hand. They all grinned broadly at each other and slapped palms. Mary Beth felt better than she had since she'd arrived at Foxhall. Finally she felt like part of the group. She had friends!

Half an hour later they were back in their beds. Mary Beth stared up at the dark ceiling above her bed, unable to sleep.

"We did it," Andie said gleefully from her corner of the room. "Ellie—alias Sarah the

115

Ghost—is safe and sound in her room."

"Well, you were right," Jina grumbled. "We've got Breakfast Club. On *Saturday* morning. And I have a show that day."

"It's no big deal," Andie said. "You'll see."

"I'm kind of disappointed it wasn't really Sarah," Lauren's voice broke in. "But that still doesn't mean the ghost doesn't exist." She paused. "So, Mary Beth, what were you saying about not being here soon? Are you trying to get kicked out of Foxhall too?"

"All right!" Andie cheered.

"No," Mary Beth said quickly. "It's just that—" She broke off, not sure what to say. How *was* she feeling about Foxhall?

"If you were going to say you're homesick, I understand," Lauren said, yawning. "It'll be okay, Mary Beth. You'll see."

"I guess so," Mary Beth murmured sleepily. But she slid her hand under her pillow to touch the envelope with the train ticket inside. It was still there, just in case she needed it. And she still couldn't decide.

14

Mary Beth stared at the picture of the bridle drawn on her quiz sheet. *Cavesson, headpiece, cheekpiece*, she wrote next to the arrows. Then her pencil froze above the last blank. What was that thing that buckled around the horse's throat?

Throatlatch, Mary Beth reminded herself, writing in the name.

It was Friday afternoon, she'd just finished the riding test, and she'd remembered the answer to every question. And that meant it was time for her to ride. Mary Beth's stomach felt queasy as she gathered her papers to hand in to Mrs. Caufield.

The director was sitting at her office desk, her muddy boots propped on a chair as she read through the quizzes. Mary Beth hesitated. This was it. If she handed in the test, she would really have to ride.

What if she fell off and Dan trampled her? He was no pony like the one who had stepped on her when she was five years old. Then, only her pelvis had been broken. This time she'd be completely smushed under Dan's big hooves.

"Mary Beth? May I have your test, please?"

With a nod, Mary Beth forced herself to walk the few steps toward Mrs. Caufield's desk. The director took the pages from her hand and glanced quickly through them. When she gave Mary Beth a big smile, Mary Beth knew for sure that she'd passed.

"Congratulations," Mrs. Caufield told her. "Now go tack Dan up."

"Yes, ma'am," Mary Beth replied. Her voice was almost a whisper.

Mrs. Caufield dropped her legs to the floor. "Listen, Mary Beth, you should be very proud of yourself. I've never seen anyone work so hard to overcome her fear of horses."

Only I haven't yet, Mary Beth said silently.

"And don't worry," the director continued. "Today you'll be on the lead line. Okay?"

"Okay." Mary Beth smiled, but as she picked up her tack and headed to Dan's stall, her legs felt like they were made of rubber.

Out of the corner of her eye she could see Jina leading Superstar down the aisle. Andie was hosing down Ranger, and Lauren was closing Whisper's stall door. Trying not to catch her roommates' attention, Mary Beth looked straight ahead. The last thing she wanted was for them to see how afraid she was.

"Need help?" Lauren was suddenly beside her, matching her stride.

"No, thanks. I think I'm okay," Mary Beth replied. But when she reached Dan's door, she dropped the saddle on it and took a deep breath. Lauren touched her on the arm.

"Hey. I know you're scared," she said. "But after last night we can get through anything, right?"

Just then Andie strode up. "You ready for the big challenge, Red?"

Mary Beth's gaze dropped to her boots.

Andie chuckled. "Hey, you can't be half as scared as I was when I saw Frawley this morning. But he just gave me the standard lecture, and cleanup detail for two weeks." She shook her head in disgust. "Now I'm going to have to think of something *really* terrible to get myself kicked out."

Mary Beth lifted her chin and looked at Andie. "You were actually scared when you saw Frawley this morning?"

"Not really." Andie grinned. "But I thought it might make *you* feel better."

Mary Beth and Lauren burst out laughing.

"What's so funny?" Jina asked, walking over to them. She was dressed in her tan schooling sweats and carrying a hunk of blue yarn in her right hand to braid into Superstar's mane.

"It's just another one of Andie's funny jokes, believe it or not," Lauren replied.

"Well, guys, I better saddle up Dan," Mary Beth said, opening the stall door.

Jina's golden eyes widened. "That's right," she said. "You're riding today."

"Don't remind me," Mary Beth said. Then she noticed that Lauren, Jina, and Andie were hiding grins and giggles behind their palms.

Mary Beth frowned. "Okay, what are you guys up to?"

"Nothing!" Lauren said innocently. "But I'd better get going. Whisper needs to be walked."

"Yeah, and I've got to finish braiding Superstar for the show tomorrow," Jina said, starting across the courtyard. "Good luck," she called over her shoulder.

Mary Beth turned to Andie. "What's going on?"

Andie held up her hands. "Hey, don't look at me. But I do want to remind you that you lost our bet. You were going to *post* at the trot by the end of the week, remember?"

Mary Beth flushed. "I guess it was pretty stupid of me to think I could trot a horse in four days."

Andie grinned. "Lucky for you, I'm a good winner. And since it looks like I'm going to be at Foxhall a little longer than I planned, you can do my homework for me for a week."

Mary Beth groaned. "Oh, that's real big of you. But you have to promise me one thing."

"Ask away," Andie said.

"When you lead me today, just *walk* Dan."

"Sure," Andie agreed easily. "I don't have any choice. After all the pranks I've pulled, Caufield's watching me like a hawk. See you in the riding ring." Andie headed down the aisle, giggling.

What's going on? Mary Beth wondered. But then she saw Mrs. Caufield coming out of her office, and she knew she didn't have time to worry about it.

Fifteen minutes later Mary Beth led Dan

into the riding ring. Mrs. Caufield was standing in the center beside Heidi and Shandra. Mary Beth couldn't believe the other beginners were grinning so happily. Even though she was pretty sure that there was no way Dan could run off with her, she couldn't shake the feeling that something horrible was going to happen.

Then she heard more laughing. Poking her head around Dan, she saw Lauren, Jina, and Andie sitting on the top rail around the ring. They were smiling and waving. Below them on the fence they'd hung a long banner that said in big letters:

WE KNOW YOU CAN
DO IT, ROOMIE!

At one end of the banner they'd drawn a giant horse. And perched on the horse's back was a tiny, red-haired girl.

They really are rooting for me, Mary Beth thought, slowly grinning back. Lauren gave her thumbs-up, and Jina called, "Good luck." Then Andie jumped off the fence rail and, lead line in hand, started walking toward her and Dan.

"Riders, mount up," Mrs. Caufield instructed.

Taking a deep breath, Mary Beth gathered up the reins. Dan swung his big head around and gazed at her with his gentle eyes.

She patted his neck. "I'm all right now, big guy. So let's do it. Let's ride."

Dear Mom, Dad, Benji, Tammy, and Reed,
Guess what I did this afternoon? I rode a horse!!! And not a pony, either. This guy is huge and his name is Dangerous Dan. But I did it, and I'm still alive.

My roommates and I are getting along okay even though Andie's still a little strange and Jina's busy being this star rider. But Lauren and I are becoming good friends.

There's tons of homework, but so far my classes are okay. I miss you all and wish Dogums was here to sleep with me. Write soon.

Love,
Mary Beth
P.S. Thanks for the train ticket. I'll save it for my first weekend visit home. See you then!

**Don't miss the next book
in the Riding Academy series:
#2: ANDIE OUT OF CONTROL**

"You could assign Magic to me!" Andie blurted out. "He's not as wild as you think. Honest!"

Mrs. Caufield and Katherine Parks, the dressage instructor, exchanged doubtful glances. Magic stood quietly, his muzzle pressed against Andie's arm.

"He just needs someone to spend time with him. You know, to build up his trust," Andie rushed on, her hand stroking the horse's neck.

Katherine raised an eyebrow and looked over at Mrs. Caufield. "Maybe she's right, Grace."

Frowning, the riding director studied Magic. Finally, she sighed and said, "All right. We'll give him two weeks."

"Yes!" Andie cried gleefully.

"But no one gets on this horse unless I say so." Mrs. Caufield pointed a finger at Andie. "And I will not tolerate your breaking any more of my rules, Ms. Perez. Check with me before you even *brush* this horse. Got it?"

"Got it," Andie replied. Magic had another chance!

**If you love horses, you'll enjoy
these other books from Bullseye:**

THE BLACK STALLION
THE BLACK STALLION RETURNS
THE BLACK STALLION AND THE GIRL
SON OF THE BLACK STALLION
A SUMMER OF HORSES
WHINNY OF THE WILD HORSES